KORY'S JUNGLE

Ann M. Jayne
Phil. 4:13

To
Madeline
&
Melina
Enjoy the
Adventure!
Ann :)

Published by Tate Publishing & Enterprises, LLC
127 E. Trade Center Terrace | Mustang, Oklahoma 73064 USA
1.888.361.9473 | www.tatepublishing.com

Tate Publishing is committed to excellence in the publishing industry. The company reflects the philosophy established by the founders, based on Psalm 68:11,
"The Lord gave the word and great was the company of those who published it."

Book design copyright © 2010 by Tate Publishing, LLC. All rights reserved.
Cover and interior design by Elizabeth A. Mason
Illustrations by Justin Stier

Published in the United States of America

ISBN: 978-1-61663-351-6
Juvenile Fiction: Fantasy & Magic
10.06.17

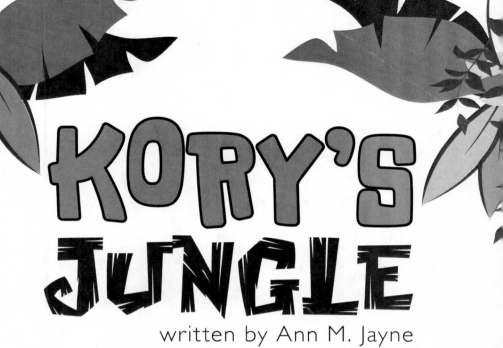

KORY'S JUNGLE

written by Ann M. Jayne

TATE PUBLISHING & Enterprises

For Ian and Justin, who truly inspire me in so many ways! I have to remember that this book would not be possible without a stuffed leopard and a little boy (and his brother) who wouldn't go to sleep!

First and foremost, I would like to thank God, above all else, for His continual love and gifts!

Thank you to my family for their support and encouragement!

Thanks go out to the 2008–2009 third grade class and their teacher, Mrs. Andrea Crabtree, at Oklahoma Christian Academy, for their enthusiasm and appreciation of this story before it became a book!

Thank you to Mrs. Teri McElroy, 4th grade teacher at Oklahoma Christian Academy, for proofreading for me before the final editing!

Thank you to the staff of Tate Publishing for believing in me!

Table of Contents

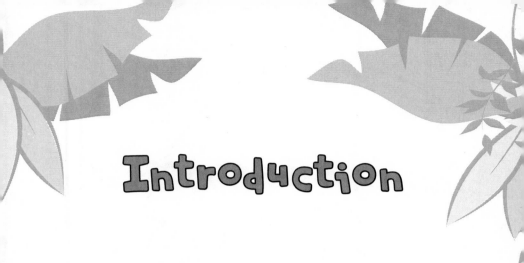

Introduction

We are all afraid of something. To others, our fears may seem trivial. How we deal with our fears—whether it's the school bully, life changes, or riding a bike for the first time without training wheels—shapes us and develops us. We must never allow our fears to make us weak; rather they must make us stronger and better. And we must remember, God is always with us, so we never have to face our fears alone.

Why?

Ian carried the last box of toys to his new room and dropped it on the floor next to the other boxes. It made a soft thud as it landed on the carpet. The lid popped open and several stuffed animals spilled onto the floor. His favorite, a leopard named Kory, was the first one to hit the floor. Ian scooped up Kory and pressed him to his chest, choking back tears.

His family had just moved to a different house, in a different neighborhood, in a different area of the city. Ian did not like it. He sat down on the floor and looked around his room. It was painted light blue and had gray carpet. His old bedroom had been painted tan and had blue carpet. His mother had painted cowboys and horses on the walls of his old bedroom. There was one window next to his closet, which was smaller than his old closet. His old room had three indows in it, and his bed had been between two of the windows. Ian could walk across his old bedroom in twelve steps. It only took him eight steps to cross his new bedroom. In his old house a bathroom connected his bedroom to the bedroom of his younger brother, Justin. Now they had to walk down the hall to the bathroom. There weren't any stairs to climb, and every room was smaller. The yard was smaller too.

Ian hugged Kory tightly, and the tears began to fall, splashing on Kory's fur. "Why did we have to move to a new house?" Ian whispered to himself. He loved the old house and missed it. The new house was so different, and Ian did not like things to be different. He heard his mother and Justin walking down the hall. Ian wiped his tears away with his sleeve. He wiped Kory off and then dried his hands on his pants.

Ian's mother put Justin in his new room and dumped a box of cars onto the floor. Justin loved cars and began making car sounds, spitting and sputtering as he drove them along the floor. Justin was four. After a while, he probably wouldn't remember the old house.

Ian knew his mother would come into his room. He tried to find something to do so she would think he was busy. He turned around to unpack another box and tripped over the box of stuffed animals he had just set down. He fell over the box onto his beanbag chair. He wasn't hurt, so he sat in the beanbag chair and stared at the floor. He hoped Mom wouldn't notice that he was upset. She did.

"What's wrong, sweetie?" Mom asked. She sat down beside Ian and smoothed his brown hair down on the right side of his head.

"I don't like it here," Ian sobbed. "I want to move back to our old house. Why did we have to move?" Ian looked up at his mother. Bigger tears welled up in his eyes and spilled down his cheeks.

Mom hugged Ian tightly. Her eyes filled with tears too. She hadn't wanted to move either and had not cried in front of Ian, because she knew it was really hard on him. She had tried to be brave for so long, and now she thought she was going to explode with sadness. Ian felt her shoulders heaving up and down. He heard her sniffle and knew she was crying, too.

"Why are you crying, Mom?" Ian asked. He had not seen his mother cry since they decided to move.

"I'm sorry, Ian," she said. "But Dad started a new job, and we have to save money. He has his own medical clinic now, and we needed to buy a smaller house so our bills will be smaller. I didn't want to move. Neither did Dad. But it was something we had to do."

"It's okay, Mom," Ian whispered. "I didn't know you and Dad were sad too. I thought you were happy that we were moving."

"I'm sad because you are sad," Mom replied. "Moving out of the house we built when you were a baby was the last thing we wanted to do. We wanted you and Justin to grow up in that house. But we have to remember that the important thing is that we are a family, no matter what house we live in."

"I guess God has a different plan for us," Ian said. He wiped his nose on his sleeve.

Mom curled up her lip. "Yuck! I don't suppose that is part of God's plan!"

Ian and Mom began to laugh. Ian felt better since he was not suffering alone.

Mom pulled a tissue out of her pocket and wiped her eyes. "Do you know what?" she said.

"What?" Ian answered.

"Tonight when Dad gets home, we are going to buy you a new bed. Justin is too big for his toddler bed, so he can have your twin bed. How about that?"

"Could I get a bunk bed?" Ian asked.

"We'll see," Mom said. "Why do you want a bunk bed? You don't have to share a room with Justin."

"I want to decorate my room like a jungle," Ian said. "The bottom bed could be my leopard cave and the top bed could be the tree that leopards climb!"

"Maybe we could hang some plastic vines on the top bed," Mom said. "That might make your room look more like a jungle."

Ian thought about it a minute. "I guess that would be cool. I could also put Exx, my stuffed snake, on the bed and wind him around in the vines." Ian spun around and jerked Exx out of the box of stuffed animals. The snake uncoiled and was almost as long as Ian.

"That's creepy!" Mom said. "Why do you want a nasty, old snake peering down on you?"

Ian giggled. "I like snakes. And spiders. Maybe I'll find a great big stuffed spider and put in on the floor."

"Oooohhhh!" Mom shivered. "I won't *ever* come in your room if you have snakes *and* spiders in here!"

Ian hugged his mom. She always made him feel better. Sometimes she could be really goofy.

"Oh, I almost forgot to tell you something," Mom said. "Tomorrow, Aunt Valerie is going to pick you and Justin up and take you to her house for a few days. Her school doesn't start until next Monday, just like your school. She wants you boys to come visit her. That way, you can have fun while I get the house straightened up."

"That will be fun," Ian said. "I better pack my bag. And I can't forget Kory."

"I already have your bag packed," Mom said. "I did it before I boxed up your clothes."

"Thanks," Ian said. He was hoping he could pack his clothes to take his mind off of school starting. He would be starting third grade at a different school, and he was scared. *What if his teacher was mean? What if all of the kids were mean and he got bullied every day? What if he couldn't do the work? What if he got lost? Or forgot his lunch?* Ian didn't realize he was so deep in thought that his forehead was furrowed.

"What's wrong?" Mom said. "You look very worried about something."

"School," replied Ian. "I'm afraid of the teacher, the kids, and not getting my work done."

"You met your teacher and she was very nice," Mom said. "I'm sure some of your friends from church will be in your class. And I know you will make many new friends. You should be excited instead of scared."

"Were you excited when you started school?" asked Ian.

"No, terrified was more how I felt," Mom said. "But it was so long ago. I do remember I learned to really like school. And my third grade teacher became one of my very favorite teachers. You'll learn to like school, too. It's just a big change for you right now. But I know you will be fine." Mom kissed Ian on the forehead and went into the kitchen to make sandwiches for lunch.

"It will be a change all right," Ian mumbled to himself. "Maybe by Monday it will rain so hard that the school will wash away! Then I won't have to go!" Deep down Ian knew that wouldn't happen. At least he could forget about it for a few days while he was at Aunt Valerie's. Hopefully.

The Coolest Bed

"Let's go eat pizza before we look for a new bed," boomed Dad's voice as he walked in the door.

Ian and Justin ran up to Dad and gave him a big hug. Then they ran out and got in the car screaming, "Pizza! Pizza! Pizza!"

Mom hugged Dad and told him Ian had had a bad day. "But I'm going to do something for him while he's at Valerie's," she said. "I hope it cheers him up." Mom whispered into Dad's ear.

"That should help," Dad said. "And I think pizza and a new bed will help too. Let's go."

As they drove to the pizza parlor, Dad asked, "What do you boys want on your pizza?"

"Cheese!" yelled Justin.

"Pepperoni!" yelled Ian.

"Worms!" yelled Mom.

"Ewwww!" yelled Ian, Justin, and Dad.

"No worms?" asked Mom. "Well, then how about hamburger?"

"That is a much better choice," said Ian. "Besides, where would they get the worms for the pizza?"

By the time they got to the restaurant, they decided to get

a small cheese pizza for Justin and a large hamburger and pep-peroni pizza for Ian, Mom, and Dad. Dad ordered the pizzas while Mom got the drinks. Ian and Justin picked out a booth and climbed in it. Ian leaned against the wall and closed his eyes, trying not to think about his old house. Justin sprinkled Parmesan cheese on his finger and then stuck his finger in his mouth. He sprinkled more cheese on his wet finger and held it up to Ian's mouth.

"Want some?" he asked.

"No thanks," Ian replied. "I'll wait for my pizza." Justin giggled and Ian smiled. Mom came back with the drinks. Dad sat down and began asking Ian what kind of bed he wanted. Ian started telling Dad about the ideas he and Mom had for his room. A few minutes later, the waitress brought the pizzas to the table.

"Here are the pizzas!" Dad said. "Who is going to say the prayer?"

"I will," said Ian. Everyone bowed their heads. "Thank you for our food, God. Thank you for my family. And thank you for—" Ian paused. He just couldn't bring himself to be thankful for his new house. "Thank you for everything. In Jesus' name, amen."

"Amen," Justin said. He grabbed a piece of pizza and shoved it in his mouth.

"So you want a bunk bed, huh, Ian?" Dad asked.

"I guess," replied Ian. "I think a bunk bed will be the best kind of leopard den. And we can also hang up plastic vines and snakes. You can't do that on a regular bed."

"Well, let's eat our pizza so we can look for you boys' new beds," Dad said. "Mom and I think Justin should get a new bed, too. We decided to sell your old bed, Ian."

"I want a fire truck bed!" Justin announced.

"A fire truck bed?" Mom asked. "So we'll have a fire station and a jungle in the same house? I guess that will work, although I've never seen a fire truck bed."

The boys gobbled up their pizza, and then everyone walked to the car.

"How long does it take to get to the furniture store, Dad?" Ian asked.

"Not too long," Dad answered. "It's just a few minutes from here."

Sure enough, they arrived at the furniture store a few minutes later. Dad parked the car.

"That was quick!" Justin said.

"It's because Dad drives so fast!" Ian informed him.

"Hey! I heard that!" Dad replied. "I just thought I'd give us more time to look at the beds! That's all." Mom rolled her eyes, and everyone laughed.

When they walked into the furniture store, a salesman named Ted introduced himself. Mom told him they were looking for children's beds. Ted led them upstairs, on an escalator, to the children's furniture showroom. Ian was amazed at the number of bunk beds there were in the showroom. He and Justin immediately began climbing up the ladder of the nearest bed.

"Cowabunga!" Justin yelled as he prepared to jump off the top bunk to another one.

"No!" Dad yelled back, grabbing Justin as he leaped off the bed. "Let's go look for your new bed while Ian decides which one he wants." Dad and Justin walked over to the twin beds. Justin immediately spied one he liked. It was a wooden bed, painted red. It had drawers, cabinet doors, and shelves on each side, just below the mattress.

"My fire truck bed!" Justin exclaimed. He began opening the drawers and doors and forgot all about the bunk beds.

Meanwhile, Ian was trying to decide which bed looked the most like a leopard den. He walked past the red and blue metal beds. They certainly didn't look like a leopard den. They were flimsy and shaky. He needed something solid and sturdy.

Then he saw the wooden beds. Some were painted green or yellow. Others were stained with a light or dark wood finish, but Ian either didn't like the color or the bed itself. His dreams of a jungle room with a leopard den began to fade.

"Let's go, Mom," Ian said sadly. "There's nothing here that looks like a leopard den." Ian grabbed Mom's hand and turned around to leave.

"A leopard den?" Ted asked. "Why didn't you say so? I have the perfect bed over here, young man. Follow me!"

Ian and Mom followed Ted around a corner. Ian stopped and stared. He couldn't believe his eyes. Right in front of him was the perfect bed. The frame of the bed was real wood, but instead of regular-looking boards, the wood had been left to look like the tree. Smaller branches spread and curved around to make up the headboard and footboard. The ladder had thick, flat rungs, and the rails looked like tree trunks. The top bunk was filled with all sorts of stuffed jungle animals. The bottom bunk had large fluffy pillows in tiger stripe print. Below the bottom bunk were three drawers. They were open and overflowing with artificial vines and leaves. Nestled in the middle drawer was a large stuffed tiger.

"*Wow!*" Ian exclaimed. "This is perfect. It's *so cool!*" He scampered up the ladder like a monkey and settled himself among the pile of elephants, zebras, and giraffes, imagining how cool his room was going to look.

Ted leaned over to Mom and whispered, "It's even on sale!"

Dad and Justin walked up. Justin announced he was getting a fire truck bed.

"Look at my cool bed," Ian proudly showed Justin.

"It's not as cool as mine," Justin snapped.

"It's cooler!" Ian snapped back.

"Enough boys!" Mom said. "You both have cool beds." She leaned over to Dad and whispered, "The really cool thing about Ian's bed is that it's on sale!"

"Great!" Dad said. "And we need one of the red twin beds over there. Let me show you." He led Ted over to Justin's fire truck bed.

"This bed is also on sale," Ted said. "What about mattresses?"

"We'll need two," Mom said. "We can use the one Ian has now for the top bunk."

"This way!" Ted said, spinning around on his heel. They walked over to the mattresses, and Ian and Justin began jumping on them.

"We both like this one!" they exclaimed together.

"Okay," said Mom.

Ted gave Dad the total price of everything. "When can we deliver them?" Ted asked.

"Friday afternoon would be fine," Mom said.

"Great!" exclaimed Ted. "I'll show you where to pay, and then you can be on your way."

After Dad paid for the furniture, they walked to the car. Ian couldn't believe that he was going to have such a cool bed. He and Justin climbed in the back seat. Mom buckled Justin into his booster seat, and Ian fastened his seat belt. As Dad drove away, he and Mom began to talk. Justin nodded off to sleep. Ian began to imagine how he was going to decorate his new bed.

"Thank you, God," Ian whispered. He smiled and started thinking about his new jungle room.

Going to Valerie's House

The next morning, Ian and Justin woke up as the sun peeped up in the eastern sky. They sprinted down the hall to Mom and Dad's room.

"We're ready to go to Valerie's!" Ian announced as loudly as he could. Mom sat straight up in bed. Dad kept on sleeping. And snoring. He had earplugs in his ears.

Mom looked at the clock. It was 7:30. "Valerie won't be here for two more hours," she said. "Go back to bed, boys."

"We aren't sleepy," Justin said. He and Ian kissed Mom and then pulled on her arm.

"How about some breakfast?" Ian asked. "Pancakes would be lovely!"

Mom and the boys giggled. Mom threw back the covers and slid her feet onto the floor. Ian and Justin grabbed her hands and led her to the kitchen.

"Okay, pancakes it is," Mom said.

While Mom rummaged around and looked for her griddle, Ian set the table. Mom found her mixing bowls and began making the pancake batter. Justin turned on the television and flopped down on the floor.

In a few minutes Mom had the first pancakes cooked. She poured the boys some orange juice and got out the syrup, maple and strawberry, while more pancakes cooked.

"Breakfast is ready!" she called. "Turn off the TV, Justin." He did and then raced Ian to the table.

"I get to say the prayer," Ian proclaimed.

"Dear God, thank you for the beautiful day and our food. In Jesus' name, amen," Justin said before Ian could even sit down.

"Mom!" Ian cried. "I wanted to say the prayer!"

"It's okay to say two prayers for breakfast," Mom said. "God doesn't mind."

"But I wanted to say it first!" Ian snarled. "Justin always does that to me! It's not fair!"

"Go ahead and say another prayer, Ian," Mom said. "You say really nice prayers."

"What about my prayers?" Justin asked.

"Yours are sweet too," Mom said. "You just need to listen to whose turn it is to pray!"

"Okay, I'll say a prayer," Ian said, bowing his head. "Dear God, thank you for our food and my family. Please let us be safe at Valerie's. In Jesus' name, amen."

Justin grabbed two pancakes with his hands and slapped them on his plate. Ian speared two pancakes with his fork and put them on his plate.

"What kind of syrup do you boys want?" Mom asked. "Maple or strawberry?" She held up both bottles and acted like she was going to pour them on the boys' heads.

"Maple for me!" Ian exclaimed. "Except I want it on my

pancakes and not on my head! I'll put strawberry syrup on my next stack of pancakes." Mom handed him the maple syrup and he poured it all over his pancakes. He cut a big piece of pancake and crammed it in his mouth.

"I want strawberry!" Justin announced. He reached up to grab the syrup from Mom's hand and almost spilled his orange juice.

"I'll pour it for you," Mom said. She poured the syrup on Justin's pancakes then cut them up in small bites. Justin stabbed a piece of pancake with his fork and shoved it in his mouth.

"*Mmmm!*" both boys said at once.

"After you finish your breakfast, you need to gather up the toys you want to take to Valerie's," Mom said. "Then brush your teeth and get dressed. After that you can watch TV until Valerie gets here."

The boys gobbled up their pancakes. Justin sprinted back to his room to pack his cars and trucks. Ian grabbed two more pancakes and poured strawberry syrup on them. Again, he cut a huge triangle of pancake and stuffed it in his mouth.

"Whubbar du donna do fy fwere don, Bom?" Ian asked.

Mom stared at him. "I didn't understand a word you said! Swallow your food before you speak, please."

Ian chewed a bit more, swallowed the massive bite of pancake, and then took a big swig of orange juice. "I said, 'What are you going to do while we're gone, Mom?'"

"Oh, Dad and I thought we'd take a little trip!" Mom teased.

"You can't do that!" Ian protested. He didn't know she was teasing, and he began to worry.

"You and Justin are going to Valerie's without me!" Mom replied.

"You can come with us!" Ian said.

"I'm just kidding, Ian!" Mom answered. "I've got to wait for the new beds to be delivered and get everything unpacked. I bet you and Justin have so much fun you won't even think about me."

"Oh, we'll think about you," Ian said. "We'll think about you while we're swimming in Valerie's pool, and eating snow cones, and staying up late watching TV!"

"Thanks!" Mom said. She leaned over and kissed Ian on the forehead. "Finish your breakfast, and then get your toys and books packed. You don't want to forget anything!"

"I'm only taking Kory, and he's riding on my lap," Ian said. "So after I get dressed and brush my teeth, I'm going to watch TV." He chewed the last bite of pancake, carried his plate to the sink, and then went to his room.

Kory was on Ian's bed. Ian put him by his bedroom door, so he wouldn't forget him. Then he made his bed. "Won't Mom be surprised?" he said to himself. Ian grabbed Kory and headed for the living room. Justin was already there watching TV. Dad was in the kitchen eating pancakes and reading the newspaper.

"Good morning, Ian," Dad said. He put the paper down and smiled at Ian. "Are you ready to go to Valerie's and leave Mom here all by herself?"

"Yep!" Ian laughed. "But she won't be alone all the time," he added. "You'll be here at night."

"That's true," Dad said. He got up and put his plate in the sink. "Give me a hug and kiss. I've got to go to work."

Ian hugged Dad and then jumped up in his arms and

smacked a big kiss on Dad's cheek. Justin ran in and gave Dad a hug too. Dad leaned down and scooped up Justin.

"My arms are full of boys!" Dad said proudly. He kissed Ian and Justin and then set them down. "Be good, boys, and have fun." Dad walked over to Mom and kissed her on the cheek. "See you tonight. I love everyone!"

"We love you too, Dad!" Mom, Ian, and Justin said at once.

Mom finished cleaning up the kitchen and then went to get dressed. By the time she was dressed, Valerie was pulling into the driveway.

"She's here!" Ian and Justin exclaimed. They pushed the front door open and ran out to meet Valerie.

"Hi, boys!" Valerie said as she got out of the car. "Are you ready to go to my house for a few days?"

"We sure are!" Justin said. He was already climbing in the car.

Mom came out with the bags and Justin's booster seat. She put it in the back seat, and he climbed onto it. Mom buckled him in, handed him his case of cars, and gave him a big hug and kiss.

"I'll miss you. I love you very much," Mom said.

"I love you too, Mom," Justin said. "Let's go Valry!"

"Hang on a minute, Justin," Valerie laughed. "I guess he won't miss you too much." Valerie laughed again, looking at Mom.

Ian ran inside to get Kory. When he came out, he gave Mom a big hug and kiss. "I'll miss you," he whispered. "I love you, Mom."

"I love you too," Mom said. "I'll miss you too, but I'll call you every night before you go to sleep, say around midnight!" Mom was teasing and ruffled Ian's hair. The horn honked and everyone looked up to see that Justin had unbuckled and climbed into the front seat to honk the car horn. Ian giggled and looked up at Mom. "Have fun swimming and staying up late," Mom said. She hugged Ian again and whispered, "When you get back, I'll have a huge surprise for you!"

"Huge?" Ian asked.

"*Huge!*" Mom answered. She walked Ian to the car. While he buckled his seat belt, she buckled Justin back into his booster seat.

"Thanks so much," Mom said to Valerie. She gave her a big hug.

"No problem," Valerie replied. "I'll bring them back Sunday after church. Have fun."

"You too," Mom said. "I'll call the boys tonight."

Mom waved to the boys. Justin waved back then began chattering to Valerie. As Valerie backed out of the driveway, Ian waved to Mom. He held up his hand, and then put down his two middle fingers, leaving his thumb, pointer and pinky finger up. He always gave Mom the "love sign" in sign language. Mom gave Ian the love sign and watched them drive down the street. She looked at her watch. She had a lot of work to do for Ian's huge surprise. It was going to be a huge surprise, indeed.

Mom Gets Busy

As soon as Mom saw Valerie's car turn off their street, she walked into the house and grabbed her purse and car keys. The night before, she had made a list of the things she needed to get. She checked to see if the list was in her purse. It was. Mom got into her car and drove to the craft and hobby store. When she got to the store, Mom grabbed a shopping basket. Then she looked at her list and put the shopping basket back. She got a shopping cart!

The first items on her list were different colors of paint. She needed green, blue, red, white, black, brown, yellow, orange, purple and pink. But when she got to the paint aisle, she was amazed at how many colors there were. Did she need Grass Green or Pea Green, Ocean Blue or Topaz Blue, Red Rage or Christmas Red? After much thought, Mom selected the colors she needed and then decided to get extra black and white to lighten or darken the colors.

"It's a good thing I got a shopping cart instead of a basket!" Mom said to herself.

She went to the next aisle and selected several sizes of paintbrushes and a few sponges too. Then she headed for the artificial flower section of the store. She selected a few large ferns and several strands of vines. She looked at the flowers, but decided Ian might not want flowers in his room.

"This should just about do it," Mom said. She paid for everything and then drove home to start to work.

When Mom got home, she moved Ian's furniture into the middle of the room. Then she covered the carpet with a large tarp. Mom placed all of the paints and brushes onto the floor and picked up a can of Tree Trunk Brown. She opened the can, dipped her brush into it, and began painting a large tree trunk next to the place where Ian's new bed would be. She painted the trunk two feet wide, and then stood on a chair to make the tree reach almost to the ceiling. Mom painted branches that spread across the whole wall.

While the paint dried, Mom ate a bologna sandwich and thought about what she would paint next. As she popped the last bit of sandwich into her mouth, she made her decision. She took a drink of water and then opened a can of golden yellow paint. Carefully, Mom began painting a leopard. "Kory" would lay on the largest branch that stretched out to where Ian's headboard would be. She painted his long tail dangling below him and green eyes that kept watch over his jungle— Ian's room.

By the time Mom finished painting Kory's spots, she heard Dad come in and walk down the hallway to Ian's room. He stood in the doorway and surveyed Mom's work.

"It looks great!" Dad said. "Ian will be surprised. He'll love it."

"I hope so," Mom said. "There is so much left to do. I've about had it for today, though. I'll get an early start on it tomorrow morning." She washed her paintbrushes while Dad took apart Ian's old bed and moved it to the garage.

For the next two mornings, Mom got up very early and began painting. While Ian and Justin slept late at Valerie's, Mom was busy painting leaves on the tree, bushes, and tall jungle grass. While Ian and Justin splashed and played in Valerie's pool, Mom painted a jungle pool and a rocky waterfall. And while the boys relaxed and watched movies, their mother painted an assortment of jungle animals: a zebra, flamingo, elephant, some monkeys, and even a tiger peering out of the bushes. And since the walls were a light blue, Mom painted some fluffy white clouds near the ceiling.

By Friday morning, Mom was finished with all of the painting. She put away the paints and brushes and folded up the tarp. The deliverymen arrived and set up the beds. After they left, Mom looked at Ian's room. The bed fit perfectly with all of the painting she had done. There was just one more thing to do.

Mom called her other sister Jennifer. She lived nearby and was coming over to help with the last bit of decorating. Then they were going shopping. Mom hung up the telephone and peeked in at Justin's room. It looked so plain compared to Ian's. Mom thought of something to do for Justin's room.

"He'll love it," she said to herself.

Jennifer arrived about ten minutes later, and she and Mom got busy. Mom arranged some of Ian's stuffed animals on his top bunk. She wound Exx through the branches of his footboard. Jennifer took the plastic ferns and nailed them on the wall where the jungle pool and rocky waterfall were painted. It looked like ferns were growing around the pool and out of the rocks of the waterfall. She nailed some of the vines on the leaves of the big tree. Some of the vines dangled down to the floor. Others looked like they were climbing up the trunk of the tree into the branches. Mom took the remaining vines and wound them through the side of the top bunk. They drooped down and partially covered Ian's bottom bunk. His bottom bunk looked like a leopard's den, indeed! When they finished everything, Mom and Jennifer stepped back and surveyed their work.

"It looks great!" Jennifer said. "Ian will flip out!"

"Yes he will," Mom replied. "I know I would have liked a room like this when I was a little girl."

"Except it would have been a horse ranch instead of a jungle!" Jennifer added. They both laughed and hugged each other.

"Thanks for your help, Jennifer," Mom said. "Come on. I'll buy you lunch before we go shopping."

"Shopping?" Jennifer asked.

"Yes," Mom answered. "I need to get new bedding for the boys' new beds. And I want to pick up some picture frames. You didn't think I would make you take off work just to work, did you?" They laughed again.

"Well, this is certainly more fun than being at work!" Jennifer added. "What pictures are you framing?"

"I took some photographs of fire trucks, police cars, tractors, and construction equipment. I had them enlarged, and I'm going to hang them in Justin's room. It looks so plain, and I don't want him to feel left out!"

"Then let's go!" Jennifer said. "I'll drive." They grabbed their purses and walked to the car. Jennifer drove to the mall. When they got there, they ate chicken sandwiches at their favorite restaurant, and then went to the department store to look for new bedding.

Mom found a chocolate brown comforter that felt like

suede (but it wasn't). "This looks like it might go well in a leopard's den, doesn't it?" she asked Jennifer.

Jennifer nodded her head in agreement. "And if Ian spills anything on it, it won't show up!"

"Exactly!" Mom said. "Now let's find something for Justin." They looked around and finally found a red and white checked comforter. "This is perfect for Justin's bed!" Mom said.

A saleswoman took the comforters and put them at the register. Mom asked her where the picture frames were and the saleswoman showed her. Mom picked out some thick metal frames. She got black, red, white, and blue frames.

"These will be great!" Mom said. She went to the register and paid for the items. Then she and Jennifer lugged the comforters and picture frames to the car.

When they got home, Mom and Jennifer began framing the photographs of the vehicles. While Jennifer put the new comforter on Ian's bed, Mom hung the photos of the fire trucks and police cars on the wall behind Justin's bed. She hung the construction equipment photos on the wall opposite Justin's bed and the photos of the tractors on the wall to the left of Justin's bed. Jennifer put Justin's new comforter on his bed. It matched perfectly! Mom and Jennifer stepped back and admired Justin's room. It was definitely a boy's room!

"I feel better," Mom said. "I don't think Justin will feel left out now."

"He'll love his room as much as Ian loves his room," Jennifer said. She looked at her watch. "I've got to get home and start supper for Rachel and Ashley," she said.

"Thanks so much for your help," Mom said. She walked Jennifer to her car and gave her a big hug. "Come over Sunday when Valerie brings the boys home so we can all visit!"

"I'll do that," Jennifer said. "I want to see the boys' faces when they see their new rooms!"

"Valerie will have them here about 1:00," Mom said. "We're going to grill hamburgers too, so come hungry!"

"See you then!" Jennifer got in her car and backed out of the driveway. Mom waved goodbye to her and went back into the house to look at the boys' rooms. She placed some of Justin's toy cars and trucks on his bookshelf. She put the bigger trucks in the cabinet underneath his bed. "Hopefully he'll keep his room looking this neat and tidy," Mom said. Then she giggled a bit, because she knew that probably would not happen! Not in a million years!

Mom walked across the hallway to Ian's room. She had done a good job with it, and the plants made it seem lifelike. Kory stared at her from the branch on his tree.

"I think this a pretty special room," Mom said. But she had no idea how special the room *really* was.

Third Grade Eve

It was Sunday. Mom and Dad went to church, and after church, they went to the grocery store to buy things for the hamburger cookout. When they got home, Dad began making the patties. Mom put the rest of the groceries away and began to set the table for the cookout. Just as she got the last plate on the table, she heard car doors slam in the driveway.

"The boys must be here!" Mom said excitedly. She and Dad hurried to the front door. Ian jerked the door open and yelled at the top of his lungs, "We're home!"

Mom put her hands over her ears. "We know. We're right here! Of course, we wouldn't have known you were here if we hadn't heard the car doors slam. You came in the house so quietly!"

Ian and Mom laughed. Mom grabbed Ian and gave him a huge hug and kiss. Dad stuck his fingers into Ian's ribs and tickled him! Laughing out loud, Ian squirmed away.

"Hey, don't I get a hug too?" Dad asked. Ian jumped into Dad's arms and squeezed him as hard as he could. "That's more like it," Dad said. He gave Ian a loud kiss on the forehead.

Just then, Justin burst through the door and announced, "Hey! I'm home!"

Once again, Mom clapped her hands over her ears. "So we've heard," she said. Then she leaned down and gave Justin a big hug and kiss. So did Dad.

Valerie and her family came in behind Justin. Her husband, Brett, was carrying the boys' suitcases and stuffed animals. Andrea and Travis, their teenage children, followed Brett into the house.

Dad grabbed the suitcases from Brett. "I sure hope they weren't this loud at your house!" he said.

"We barely knew they were there!" Valerie laughed.

Ian and Justin raced off to their rooms, but before they got too far, Mom yelled, "*Stop!*"

They both stopped and looked back at her. "Why?" they asked at once.

"You have to put these on," Mom said, holding up two blindfolds. "You each have a huge, and I mean *huge*, surprise in your rooms."

Dad bent down to tie on the blindfolds. He led Justin to his room and Mom led Ian to his. Valerie, Brett, Andrea, and Travis followed behind, eager to see the huge surprise too.

"Ta da!" Mom said to the boys as she and Dad pulled off their blindfolds.

Ian looked at his room. He rubbed his eyes in disbelief. His eyes wandered around the room, taking in the sights. They stopped when he saw the leopard painted on the wall. The leopard seemed to be looking right at Ian.

"Wow!" Ian exclaimed. "This is perfect!" Ian ran over to Mom and gave her a hug. "I *love* my room, Mom!" Ian exclaimed. "You did a great job. It looks better than I imagined!"

"I'm glad you like it," Mom said. She gave Ian another hug and then left him to see how Justin was doing. "How do you like your room, Justin?" Mom asked. Justin was putting his monster trucks on the shelves below his bed.

"It's great!" he said, without even looking at Mom.

"Do you like the pictures?" Mom asked.

"Yes!" Justin said. "I wish I could ride on a fire truck just like that one." Justin pointed to one of the photos.

"Maybe you can some day," Mom answered. She leaned down and kissed Justin. He was busy arranging his trucks in a straight line on the shelf when he heard the doorbell ring.

"That must be Jennifer, or Grandy and Pappy," Mom said. Before she could turn around to leave Justin's room, he and Ian had sprinted down the hall to see who was at the door.

It was Jennifer, her girls, *and* Grandy and Pappy. Grandy and Pappy were Mom's parents. Dad's parents, Grammy and Popu, would be over in a few minutes.

"Come see our rooms!" Ian exclaimed as he grabbed Pappy's hand and led him down the hall. Justin grabbed Grandy's hand, and they followed Ian and Pappy. Rachel and Ashley followed them, and Jennifer went too because she wanted to watch the boys in their new rooms.

Pappy liked the fish painted in the jungle pool. "I'd like to fish there," Pappy said. He sat down in the floor, and he and Ian began thinking of names for the animals. They named the zebra "Checkers," the elephant "Tiny," and the flamingo "Blackie."

"I better go see Justin's room," Pappy said. "Let's think of more names in a minute."

"Okay, Pappy," Ian said.

Pappy went to Justin's room and got down on the floor to play cars with him. He told Justin all about the engines of the cars and trucks and how they worked. He and Justin made sputtering noises as they drove the cars and trucks.

Grandy went into Ian's room. Ian told her the names of the animals he and Pappy had thought of, and Grandy laughed. "Pappy's silly, isn't he?" she said.

"Yes, he is," Ian giggled.

At the sound of the doorbell, Justin left Pappy in his room and raced to the front door.

"Come in, come in!" he exclaimed to Grammy and Popu. "You two have got to come see my room!" He took Grammy's hand and led her down the hallway. Popu followed them. "Oh, and Ian's room too." Justin added.

Dad announced that the hamburgers were ready to eat. Everyone gathered around the kitchen table and held hands while Dad said the prayer. Then they munched on hamburgers and crunched on potato chips. Grammy had brought a cake, and while everyone was eating their hamburgers, Justin scraped icing off the cake with his finger. He licked the icing off his finger, and then scooped away some more. After several mouthfuls of icing, he began to eat his hamburger.

Mom noticed icing around Justin's mouth. She looked over at the cake and gasped, "Oh no!" when she saw the cake. Everyone stopped eating and looked at Mom. Justin tried to wipe the icing off his mouth.

"What happened?" Grammy asked.

"Some of the cake icing has mysteriously disappeared," Mom declared. "Did anyone see the icing thief?" Justin giggled and raised his hand.

"You saw the icing thief?" Dad asked.

"Yes, it was Rascal!" Justin declared.

"I don't see any paw prints," Mom said.

"That's because Rascal licked them up!" Justin laughed. So did everyone else.

"Don't you need to apologize to Grammy and everyone else?" Mom asked Justin.

Justin hung his head and said softly, "Sorry for eating the cake icing."

"Now, Justin," Dad said, "since you've already had plenty of icing, no cake for you!"

"All right," Justin said quietly. For dessert, everyone except Justin ate some icing-less cake and sat around to talk for a while. Then it was time for everyone to leave, since the next day was a workday. And school day. When Ian thought about going to school, he felt his stomach fill with butterflies and knots.

Pappy hugged him good-bye. He noticed the worried look on Ian's face. "What's wrong?" he asked.

"I'm *really* nervous about school tomorrow," Ian replied. He hugged Pappy as tightly as he could.

"School will be fine," Pappy said. "Your mom used to get nervous before school, but by the second day she was fine. Just don't be like your Aunt Valerie. She used to throw up the night before school started!"

"Ewww!" Ian said. "I hope I don't get *that* nervous!"

Pappy squatted down and looked Ian in the eyes. "Don't worry about school, Ian," he said. "I know you will be the smartest boy in the classroom. And the nicest." Ian managed a weak smile.

"And just think," Pappy added, "tomorrow at this time the first day of school will be over, and you'll realize there was nothing to worry about." Ian squeezed Pappy's hand. Pappy stood up and his knees made a loud *crack*. Ian laughed. So did

Pappy. "See," Pappy said. "You may be worried about school, but at least you don't have to worry about your knees popping like corn when you bend down or stand up!"

They laughed again, and Grandy walked up to hug Ian. "I might just have to get the school boy a special treat," she said.

By the time everyone hugged each other, said their good-byes, hugged each other again, and then left, it was time for Ian and Justin to take a bath and go to bed.

Justin was tired. He took a quick bath, put on his pajamas, and grabbed a bedtime story for Mom to read. Ian tried to make his bath last as long as he could. He did not want to go to bed. He did not want to lie there and think about school starting tomorrow.

"Ian, it's time to get out of the bath tub," Dad said. "Brush your teeth too."

As Ian rinsed the shampoo out of his hair, he opened the drain. He finished rinsing his hair and watched the water swirl down the drain, like a teeny tornado. He wished his worries would disappear like the water down the drain. But when the bathtub was empty, Ian still had a head, and tummy, full of worries. He dried off, put on his pajamas, and brushed his teeth. Ian walked slowly into the living room. Mom was reading the last page of Justin's story to him. Justin yawned and rubbed his eyes.

"It's time for prayers, boys," Dad said. "Who is going to pray first?"

"I will. Dear God, thank you for the beautiful day and my family. In Jesus' name, amen." Justin had answered and said his prayer before Ian had a chance to respond!

Normally, this would have made Ian mad. But not tonight.

"I want to say my prayer last," Ian mumbled. "Mom, would you and Dad pray that I don't worry about school?"

"Of course we will," Mom answered. Ian slid next to her and she rubbed his back as she said her prayer. Then Dad said his prayer. Both of them asked God to help Ian stop worrying and have a good day at school.

Now it was Ian's turn to pray. He took a deep breath and closed his eyes. He started thinking about his old house and how he knew he wouldn't be as worried about school if he was in his old room. Well, his old room that looked as cool as his new room. He was thinking about so many things, he forgot to say his prayer.

Mom nudged Ian.

"Dear God," Ian began, "please let me not worry about school and have a good day at school tomorrow. In Jesus' name, amen."

Justin sprinted back to his room, so he could hide under the covers. He did this every night, but always seemed amazed that Dad and Mom found him—after they looked in the closet and behind the door and under his train set of course!

While Dad and Mom went to "look" for Justin, Ian shuffled slowly back to his room. He climbed into his new bed, which, under normal circumstances, would have been very exciting. But with third grade looming ahead, he realized that he was terrified. He hugged Kory as tightly as he could.

Mom and Dad tucked Justin in bed, gave him a "million" kisses, and then came in to tuck Ian in his bed. Dad gave Ian a "million" kisses and then went to take a shower.

"Good night, Ian," Mom whispered as she leaned down to give Ian his "million" kisses. She wrapped the vines around his bunk bed ladder.

"Mom?" Ian asked softly.

"Yes, Ian," answered Mom.

"I'm *really* scared about starting school tomorrow." Ian looked up at Mom. Even though it was cozy and dark in his bed, the hall light shone through enough into Ian's room that Mom could see Ian's eyes glistening with big tears.

Mom sat on Ian's bed and gave him a hug. "It will be all right, Ian."

"Do you promise?" Ian asked as a large single tear slid down his right cheek. He wiped it away as his lips began to tremble.

"I promise," Mom answered firmly. "Just enjoy your first night in your new bed in your cool, new room. And remember, tomorrow night at this time, your first day of school will be over. You'll probably be wondering why you worried so much about it."

"That's what Pappy said," Ian said.

"Well, he helped calm my fears before school started," Mom said.

Ian gave Mom a hug and said, "I love you, Mom."

"I love you too," Mom answered. She patted Ian on the chest, stood up, and walked out of his room. Ian rolled onto his left side and looked around his room, clutching Kory tightly. He saw Checkers, Tiny, and Blackie. He stared at the painted Kory until his eyes grew heavy. He rolled onto his back and cradled Kory in his arms. Slowly Ian closed his eyes, trying not to think about tomorrow. He squeezed his eyes tighter and tighter, hoping that would squeeze the thoughts of school out of his head. In a few minutes, Ian grew tired of squeezing his eyes. He let them relax for a minute, and as his eyes relaxed, so did his body and his mind.

Ian was almost asleep when he felt a thump on his chest.

Kory's Jungle

He opened his eyes with a start. Ian could not believe what he saw, and what he saw made him gasp for breath.

Ian Meets Kory

Ian was staring straight into the green eyes of a leopard! It was standing on its hind legs silently twitching its long velvety tail, and had its front paws on Ian's chest. The leopard moved his head toward Ian's face. He touched Ian's nose with his nose. His whiskers brushed Ian's face.

"Hello, Ian," the leopard said. "I'm Kory."

Ian was almost too terrified to speak, but managed to squeak out "Uh, h-h-h-hello." Ian felt the stuffed Kory under his arm. *Where did this leopard come from?* Ian wondered. *Is he going to eat me?* At the same time, he couldn't help but notice how strikingly beautiful the leopard was. His fur was a golden yellow, like honey in the sunshine. The leopard's spots were like splotches of black ink. His paws were huge, bigger than Dad's hands, yet they were so light and soft that Ian could barely feel them on his chest. Staring at the leopard, Ian summoned up enough courage to ask, "Where did you come from?"

"From there," Kory said, looking toward the wall with the tree and leopard painted on it.

Ian craned his neck around to see where Kory was looking. He saw the painted tree, *but there was no painted leopard in the tree!* Ian looked back at the leopard. "Are you the painted

Kory?" he asked. *But how could he be?* Ian wondered. This leopard was real, *alive,* like the ones he had seen in the zoo or on nature programs.

"Yes," Kory replied. "That's me. That's my tree. And I would like to show you my jungle."

"But I can see your jungle," Ian replied. "My mom painted it. It's really cool."

"It sure is," agreed Kory. "But I want to show you my *real* jungle. I want to *take* you to it. Climb on my back."

"Huh?" Ian grunted. He thought he must be dreaming. He rubbed his eyes and sat up.

Kory was standing on all four legs by Ian's bed, facing the painted tree. He looked at Ian and said again, "Climb on my back."

Ian pushed the covers back. He slid his left foot onto the floor, and then his right foot. He stood up very slowly and cautiously. *This is really weird,* he thought. Carefully he lifted his right leg over Kory's left shoulder. When that foot touched the floor on the other side of Kory, Ian scooted his bottom down onto Kory's sleek back.

"Hang on!" Kory said.

"To what?" Ian asked.

But there was no answer. Kory crouched down and leaped toward the painted tree—the painted tree that used to have a painted leopard in it. Ian grabbed the fur behind Kory's shoulders. He gripped Kory's ribs with his legs and closed his eyes. *This is going to hurt when I smack into the wall,* Ian thought. He kept his eyes tightly closed, and his jaws clenched shut, bracing for the unpleasant contact with the wall. But in the next instant, he felt Kory land on something sturdy and solid. Ian

still had his eyes shut, but heard birds squawking and monkeys hooting.

"You can open your eyes now," Kory said. "We're here."

Ian opened his right eye, realized he wasn't unconscious from slamming into the wall, and then opened his left eye. He and Kory were in a tall, leafy tree on a thick, round branch high above the ground. Ian looked around and saw treetops everywhere. He relaxed his grip on Kory and sat up straight. Monkeys and parrots and cockatoos were in these trees, chattering and squawking. He saw birds flying in the air and looked down in time to see a zebra trot by. Its hooves made a soft clip-clopping noise as it trotted into the jungle. Ian also noticed that he wasn't wearing his pajamas, either! He was wearing denim shorts, an orange tee shirt, and sneakers.

"Where am I?" Ian asked Kory.

"You're in my jungle," Kory answered matter-of-factly, as though Ian went there all of the time. "Let me show you around. Hang on tight. We're going down!"

Ian clenched Kory's fur with his hands and wrapped his legs around Kory's ribs.

"Down we go!" Kory exclaimed. He lunged off the branch and landed on a branch several feet below them.

"Keep hanging on until we're on the ground," Kory told Ian. But before Ian could answer, "Don't worry," Kory hopped nimbly down from branch to branch. He looked back at Ian and asked him if he was okay. Ian nodded, and with that, Kory made one final leap, gliding past four more branches until he landed softly on the ground. Shaking a bit, Ian slid off Kory's back, grateful to be on solid ground. The floor of the jungle was soft, brown dirt covered with cool, green moss, leaves, and grass.

"Wow!" Ian exclaimed. "This is incredible!"

"You've just seen a little bit of my jungle," Kory said. "Come on. Let's go meet some of my friends."

They started walking on a well-trodden jungle path. Tall trees towered over them. But none of the trees were as tall as the tree they had jumped out of. Kory walked soundlessly through the jungle. Ian managed to step on nearly every twig on the ground, crunching and snapping them like crisp strips of bacon.

"Sorry I'm making so much noise, Kory," Ian said. "I've never been in a real jungle before. It's amazing!"

"I enjoy it," Kory said. "And don't worry about the noise. I'm not hunting for anything to eat. Yet."

They continued walking, and Ian continued stepping on twigs that were on the path. Suddenly a huge snake dropped his head down right in front of Ian! The rest of his long body was wrapped around the branch of a tall tree. The snake flicked its tongue and tickled Ian's nose. It was a boa constrictor!

"*Aauugghh!*" Ian screamed. He jumped sideways, falling over Kory. He landed on his bottom with his feet and hands splayed out around him. The snake unwound from the tree and slithered over to Ian, who was ready to crab walk away as fast as he could go.

Kory, not in the least bit alarmed that a huge snake had just appeared or that Ian had nearly knocked him down, looked calmly at Ian and said, "Ah, here's one of my friends now."

"My name is Exx," the snake said to Ian. "Who are you?" His tongue flickered at Ian and his yellow, beady eyes stared intently into Ian's blue eyes.

Ian scrambled to his feet. Now that he knew he was not going to be squeezed to death, he held out his right hand to shake hands with Exx. "I'm Ian," he said, then quickly dropped his hand to his side, because he forgot for a moment that snakes don't have hands. He didn't want to appear rude, since this was his first introduction to a real, live boa constrictor.

"Welcome to the jungle, Ian," hissed Exx.

"Thank you," Ian said. Since his heartbeat was returning to normal, Ian noticed what a beautiful snake Exx was. Exx had light tan skin with black *X*s winding along it, like a really long shoelace. Dark brown spots splattered on each side of the *X*s. Ian reached out his left hand to touch Exx. He ran his hand lightly along Exx's long back and noticed the way the snake-skin felt. It felt smooth, but also just a tiny bit bumpy, sort of like rubbing his arm or leg when he had goose bumps! "You are a very beautiful snake," Ian said. "I've never been this close to a real, live snake before." (He had been close to a real *dead* snake when his dad killed one slithering through the yard, but he thought it would be best if he didn't mention that tidbit of information to Exx.)

"Thank you," Exx replied. "I've never been this close to a real, live human before either. I was afraid you might be a mean, little boy!"

"I like snakes," Ian said. "Would you like to go with Kory and me? Kory is going to show me more of the jungle."

"No, thank you," Exx replied. "Perhaps I will do it another time. I haven't eaten in several days, so I need to get back in my tree and catch a bird, or monkey, or something."

Ian gulped at the thought of some pretty bird or cute chattering monkey meeting such a gruesome fate. But, he was glad it wasn't him!

"Well, good-bye then, Exx," Ian said. "It was nice meeting you."

"Likewise," hissed Exx. He nodded at Ian, then wound himself around the trunk of the tree and slid up the tree to wait for his lunch.

"Are *you* hungry, Ian," Kory asked.

"A little," said Ian. "What did you have in mind?" He wondered if Kory was going to offer him raw zebra meat for his jungle snack.

"It's a real treat," Kory said. "But don't worry. I won't make you eat a zebra on your first visit to the jungle!"

Ian breathed a small sigh of relief and followed Kory down the path. Kory didn't make a sound as he padded along on the path. Ian had to dodge low-hanging limbs and push back bushes as he followed Kory. He still managed to step on a few twigs.

Finally the trees and bushes gave way to a beautiful clearing. Ian stepped out from the bushes and gazed at a crystal clear jungle pool. He could see shiny silvery fish darting around. A huge waterfall rained into the pool. On the left side of the pool were several brilliant green bushes taller than Ian. They were covered with plump purple berries. A brightly beaked toucan was perched on one of the bushes, plucking berries off and tossing them down his throat.

"Have a berry or two," Kory told Ian.

Ian reached out and plucked a fat berry off a bush. Slowly he put it in his mouth and crunched down on it. Thick, juicy syrup filled his mouth and a sweet flavor like the sweetest cherries and blueberries hit his taste buds.

"These are delicious!" Ian announced. He plucked more berries off the bush and stuffed them in his mouth. Juicy berry syrup dribbled down his chin. Ian tucked his chin sideways and wiped his chin on his shirtsleeve. He ate a few more berries and then stuffed some in one of the pockets of his shorts. A drop of purple juice was dangling off Ian's chin.

"What are these berries called?" he asked Kory.

"Buffalo berries," Kory replied.

"Buffalo berries?" questioned Ian. "Because they are so big?" Ian popped two berries into his mouth and waited for Kory to answer. But Kory was standing very still. His right ear was cocked back. He was listening to something.

Ian thought Kory didn't hear him, so he repeated his question. "Because they are so—"

"Shhh!" Kory said quickly.

Ian stopped chewing his berries. He heard a rumbling and crashing sound coming from the jungle path they had just been on.

"Get out of the way!" Kory roared. He bounded toward Ian, grabbed his shirt collar in his mouth, and jumped up to a large rock hanging out over the waterfall. As Ian's feet touched the rock, he and Kory turned around just in time to see four large water buffaloes crash into the clearing. They stomped over to the buffalo berry bushes and began gobbling up the berries, snorting and smacking as they ate.

Kory looked at Ian and whispered, "*That's* why they are called buffalo berries! And believe me, we are much safer up here than down there. You never, *ever* want to get between a water buffalo and buffalo berries. *Always* remember that the water buffaloes are the jungle bullies!"

Ian nodded in agreement. "I'll remember that," he whispered to Kory, hoping he would never come face-to-face with a water buffalo.

Ian and Kory watched the water buffaloes eat, eat, and eat. They smacked and snorted and chomped. Finally the water buffaloes filled up on berries and waddled over to the pool where they slurped up water. The shiny silver fish darted to the other side of the pool. After the water buffaloes quenched their thirst, the largest one tramped off into the jungle. The other three started after him. But before the last one left, he shook his head and sent purple buffalo berry slobber flying in all directions. Some of it landed on Kory and Ian.

"Yuck," Ian said softly. Even though the slobber was gross, he sure didn't want to yell and make the water buffaloes come back. He and Kory climbed down from the rocks. It was a good thing Ian had put some berries in his pocket, because the only berries left were the ones that were squished on the ground or the green ones that weren't ripe.

"I should take you back to my tree," Kory said. He headed for the jungle path that they had followed to the pool and berry bushes.

"But I'm not ready to go," Ian said. "This is really exciting."

"You can come back again," Kory replied. "But right now it's not safe with those water buffaloes roaming around. They would just love to stomp on someone! Let's go."

Ian followed Kory back to the tree. He listened to the birds and monkeys as he walked along, his hand running up and down Kory's sleek back. Surprisingly, he didn't step on many twigs.

When they reached the tallest tree in the jungle, Kory told Ian to climb on his back and hang on. Ian wrapped his legs tightly around Kory's ribs and grabbed some fur behind Kory's shoulders. Kory pushed off the ground with his powerful hind legs. He landed on a branch, looked back to make sure Ian was still there (he was), and jumped up to the next branch. Each time he landed on a new branch, he made sure Ian was still with him. Kory stopped on the ninth branch.

"Okay, Ian," he said. "We're here. I'll take you back to your room so hang on one more time."

Ian closed his eyes as Kory leaped toward the big thick tree trunk. Ian felt Kory land and opened his eyes. He was back in his room and in his pajamas. He slid off Kory's back and climbed into bed.

Kory grabbed the bed covers with his mouth and pulled them up around Ian, tucking him in. Ian put his hands on Kory's cheeks and looked into Kory's green eyes.

"I had a marvelous time," he told Kory. "Thank you so much for taking me to your jungle." Ian stroked Kory's head and Kory began to purr.

"I'll come back again," Kory purred to Ian. "Perhaps next time you can stay longer and meet more of my friends. Good-bye, Ian."

"Good-bye, Kory!" Ian whispered. He rubbed his eyes, realizing he was suddenly tired. When Ian stopped rubbing his eyes, Kory was gone! He looked at the tree and saw the painted Kory lying in the tree.

What a wild dream, Ian thought. He rolled over and immediately fell asleep.

Third Grade

Ian slept so peacefully all night that he didn't hear Mom telling him to wake up. She opened the blinds, letting sharp morning sunlight fill Ian's room. Ian squinted and then burrowed his head under the covers.

"Time to get up, Ian," Mom said, pulling the covers off him. "You don't want to be late for your first day of school!"

Ian's eyes flew open. *School!* He jumped out of bed and jerked open one of his dresser drawers. He grabbed a pair of denim shorts and an orange tee shirt. He pulled off his pajamas and put on his clothes. Then he went to the bathroom and brushed his teeth. He could feel his stomach begin to twist and knot up, but it wasn't as bad as it had been last night. Then he remembered Kory and his trip to the jungle. What a vivid dream!

Ian walked into the kitchen. Mom had bacon and toast ready. Ian really didn't feel like eating, but nibbled on a crisp bacon strip anyway. Mom kissed him on the forehead and then went to wake up Justin. They were all taking Ian to school.

Dad came in and poured a cup of coffee. He sat down by Ian and snatched a piece of Ian's bacon. "Nervous?" he asked Ian.

"Sort of," Ian said. "I was thinking about this really weird dream I had last night."

"Tell me about it," Dad said.

"He'll have to in the car," Mom said. She packed some bacon and toast for Justin to eat in the car. "Let me take your picture, Ian. Then we need to go."

Mom hustled Ian over to the fireplace and snapped a few pictures. Then she decided some outdoor photos would be nice, so they went onto the back porch. Rascal, Ian's beagle, came bounding up to see Ian. He was wagging his tail so hard that everything from his shoulders to the tip of his tail was twisting back and forth. Baloo, their Great Pyrenees, came trotting up to see Ian too. Mom snapped a few photos of Ian with the dogs. "Okay, now we need to get you to school," Mom told Ian. She opened the back door, and Rascal darted into the kitchen.

"You can't go to school, Rascal," Dad said. Ian grabbed dog treats for Rascal and Baloo. Rascal happily followed Ian outside and gobbled up his treat.

Justin staggered into the kitchen. He was still sleepy and was rubbing his eyes. He had his shirt and shorts with him. "Let's get you dressed, Justin," Dad said, taking a big swig of coffee. He stripped off Justin's pajamas and slid on his shirt that had a fire truck on it. Justin stepped into his shorts and put on his sandals.

Mom grabbed Justin's bacon and toast as well as a cup of orange juice. Then everyone got in the car, and Dad drove to Ian's school. When they got to the school, Dad parked the car, and everyone went to Ian's room. Mom brought her camera so she could take a picture of Ian at his desk.

Mrs. Land was waiting in her classroom for everyone to

arrive. She had decorated their room like a farm. Posters of tractors, fields, barns, and farm animals were on the wall. There were four groups of desks with four desks in each group. The front of the desks were pushed together to form a big rectangle, two on one side and two on the other side, so the kids would face each other.

"Welcome to third grade, Ian!" Mrs. Land exclaimed. She gave Ian a big hug. "Here, you can pick where you want to sit."

Ian looked around the room. Three other students and their parents came in, so Ian hurried and put his backpack at the desk nearest Mrs. Land's desk. *At least I'll be close to the teacher if someone is mean to me,* Ian thought.

Mom snapped a picture of Ian at his desk. Dad bent down on one knee and put his arm around Ian. Justin stood on the other side of Ian, and Mom snapped a picture of them. Then she and Dad traded places, and he took a picture of Mom and Ian. Justin decided to look around the room rather than have his picture taken again.

The classroom was beginning to buzz with noise as students and their parents and siblings came in. A pretty girl named Ginger came in and sat next to Ian. She had long black hair that was pulled back into a ponytail. It was tied with a pink ribbon, which matched her pink dress, pink socks and pink shoes. She got a pink pencil out of her pink pencil box—which was in her pink backpack—placed the pencil on her desk, and smiled at Ian. Ian smiled back. Then, to his relief, he saw Tristan and Jamie, his friends from church, walk in the room.

"Over here!" Ian called to them. Tristan and Jamie came over and sat with Ian and Ginger. As they put their backpacks on their desks, Mom told Ian, "See, you have some friends here already! There's nothing to worry about."

More students arrived, and Ian noticed there was one other friend from church, Reed, in his class. Reed was sitting with three girls. They were giggling at him, because he was sticking his tongue out at them. Ian waved to Reed, and he waved back with his tongue sticking out of his mouth. Ian noticed that one of the girls was really pretty.

Now it was time for the parents to leave. Dad and Justin hugged Ian. "Be good," Dad said, kissing Ian on the forehead. Justin really wanted to stay, but Dad led him out to the car.

Justin pulled back on Dad's hand yelling, "*I want to stay and play with the kids!*"

Ian and Mom giggled. "It will be fine," Mom said. "I've got to go. Dad has to take Justin and me home before he goes to work. I'll see you at three o'clock. I love you." She hugged Ian but when she tried to leave, Ian wouldn't let go. Mom had to pry him off of her, like someone trying to wiggle out of pants that are too tight. She gave Ian the love sign, and he returned it.

After the parents left, Mrs. Land shut the door. She began to explain how everyone should hang up their backpacks and where to put their lunchboxes. There was a chart with two columns labeled "Brought My Lunch" and "Ordered a School Lunch." The kids would move a magnetic farm animal with their name on it to the appropriate column. Then Mrs. Land had every student stand up and say his or her name.

Ian paid attention as the students introduced themselves, particularly the really pretty girl. Her name was Mollie. The last student to stand up was a large boy about twice Ian's size, as well as all of the other kids in class. He had black hair, but it was cut so short he looked like a sheep that had been sheared.

"My name's Douglas, but everybody better call me *Doug!*" he snarled. His eyes narrowed, and he looked right at Ian.

Great, Ian thought. *He hates me, and I don't even know him!* Doug clenched his fist as a reminder to warn everyone in case they forgot and called him Douglas.

"Okay, uh, Doug," Mrs. Land said. "We need to remember to be polite to our new friends." She patted him on the shoulder and walked back to her desk. Doug sat down, but continued to glare at Ian, then Ginger, then whoever else looked at him.

Mrs. Land told everyone to take out their crayons and draw a picture of themselves doing their favorite activity. Ian drew himself playing with Rascal.

"Doug is probably drawing a picture of himself beating up a kid," Ian whispered to Tristan. Tristan snickered.

"Yeah," Tristan replied, "or pulling legs off a grasshopper!"

When everyone was finished, Mrs. Land collected the papers and showed each one to the class. "This will help you learn something about your new friends," she said happily. She showed a picture of Reed playing football, Tristan painting a picture, Jamie playing tennis, and Ginger shopping with her Mom. Of course, Ginger had colored everything in her picture pink. Other pictures showed kids riding horses, reading books, and swimming. But Doug's picture showed him eating an ice cream cone. Next to him, he had drawn a little boy who was crying.

Mrs. Land tried to be positive. "Why, Doug, what is your favorite kind of ice cream?"

She hoped he would say vanilla, chocolate, or strawberry, but Doug said coldly, "Whatever flavor I get from any other kid."

"Well, Doug," Mrs. Land added, "we need to remember to be nice to our friends." She managed to smile, but quickly realized she had the bully of the elementary school right here in her classroom. Doug scowled at her and then directed his scowl to Ian and Ginger. Ian hurriedly began putting his crayons back in their box.

When it was time for lunch, Ian made it his mission to sit between Reed and Tristan, putting as much space between himself and Doug as possible. Everyone else seemed to have the same idea as they were all bunched together on one end of the table! Mrs. Land sat down by Doug and then invited Mollie and a boy named Alan to join them. Ian said a silent prayer of thanks that Mrs. Land hadn't chosen him to sit by Doug.

After lunch it was time for recess. Ian, Reed, Tristan, and Jamie headed for the monkey bars. They were soon joined by Mollie, Alan, and Ginger. Ian scanned the playground to see where Doug was. He saw him standing by a chain link fence that separated the playground from the neighboring houses. Doug was throwing gravel at a little, brown, fuzzy dog. The dog yelped and ran to the other side of its yard. Doug threw more gravel at the dog, laughing the whole time.

"Look at what Doug is doing!" Ian told his friends, pointing at Doug. They all stopped and looked to where Ian was pointing.

"Oh, that poor, little dog," Mollie moaned. "Someone should tell Mrs. Land."

"Yeah, so Doug can beat the crud out of whoever snitches on him," Reed stated. "Not me!"

Mrs. Land was busy with a girl who had fallen and scraped her knee. She had her back to the fence and didn't see Doug.

Ian gulped. Should he tell Mrs. Land? If he hurried, maybe Doug wouldn't see him talking to her. But if he did—well, Ian really didn't feel like having the crud beaten out of him! He didn't want to be a snitch, but he didn't want the little dog to get hurt either.

Just then, Ian and his friends heard a whistle blow. Another teacher, Miss Denton, had spotted Doug and was marching over to him. Ian watched her talk to Doug, pointing her finger at him and then the little dog. Ian didn't know what she was saying to Doug, but Doug stopped throwing rocks at the dog. Miss Denton led Doug away from the fence and then pointed to all of the things that he could play with on the playground. To Ian's horror, Miss Denton pointed to the monkey bars where he and his friends were! And at this very moment, they happened to be watching Doug! Everyone turned away quickly, acting as if nothing had happened. But Doug's eyes met Ian's. Doug clenched his teeth and snarled at Ian. Ian flipped over the monkey bars, acting as if he hadn't seen Doug threaten him.

Great, Ian thought, *I'm going to get creamed by Doug on the first day of school!* Doug walked over to a tree and sat down and Ian breathed a sigh of relief.

"Can you believe someone got into trouble on the first day of school?" Ginger asked.

"It'll probably happen on the second day, and third day, and fourth day, and ..." Jamie added.

Everyone laughed. Mrs. Land blew her whistle and told her class to line up to go back inside. Ian jumped off the monkey bars and raced across the playground to be the first one behind Mrs. Land. *I'll be safe there,* he thought. Reed filed in behind Ian, and he felt better. Reed was much taller than Ian, so Ian knew Doug couldn't see him!

The rest of the day was fairly uneventful. Mrs. Land

explained their daily schedule and told them they would sit with their group at lunch from now on. Mrs. Land handed out a coloring sheet, and then they had another recess. Doug did *not* throw rocks at the little, brown dog this time. After recess, they colored on their coloring sheets and ate a snack. Soon it was time to go home.

Ian was so relieved that he hadn't been creamed by Doug on his first day of school! He couldn't wait for Mom to get there, so he could tell her all about Doug. While he waited for her, he finished coloring the picture Mrs. Land had given him. When he was finished, he looked up and saw Mom and Justin walking through the door. He stuffed his crayons in the box and put the box in his desk. He grabbed his backpack and hurried to the door.

"My, that was quick!" Mom exclaimed as Ian hugged her.

"He had a great day," Mrs. Land told Mom. "I'll see you tomorrow, Ian." Mrs. Land gave Ian a hug, and then Ian, Mom, and Justin left.

"My first day of school is *over!*" Ian exclaimed to Mom. He chattered to her the whole way home, telling her about the events of the day, especially elaborating on the part where Doug threw rocks at the little, brown dog and got caught by Miss Denton. When Dad got home, Ian relayed the stories of his first day of school to Dad, as well as to his grandparents, aunts, and uncles who all called to see how his first day of school had been.

When it was time for bed, Ian was surprised at how tired he was. Mom and Dad kissed him good night. After they left, Ian remembered what Pappy and Mom had told him last night, "Tomorrow at this time, the first day of school will be over, and you'll realize there was nothing to worry about."

They were right! Ian wasn't worried, except for a slight gnawing at his stomach when he thought about Doug. Other than that, third grade was a piece of cake! He briefly thought about Kory, but realized he must have just had a wild dream. Ian mumbled a silent prayer of thanks and drifted off to sleep without a worry in his head.

Bad News and Buffaloes

The next couple of weeks passed quickly, and Mrs. Land's class settled into their routine. For Ian, school had gone fairly well. He had tried to avoid any contact with Doug, but on a couple of occasions, Doug had made Ian give up his turn at the swing, which made everyone else leave the swings, or Doug had cut in front of Ian in the lunch line. Ian had seen Doug grab Ginger's cookies out of her lunch box and take Tristan's juice.

Doug's group sat next to Ian's group at lunch. Ian noticed that Doug was always by himself on the playground, and no one ever talked to him at lunch.

No wonder, he thought, *since he steals cookies and juice and turns at the swing.* Ian almost felt sorry for Doug, but at the same time, he was terrified of Doug and knew the other kids were too. It made Ian feel better knowing that he wouldn't be considered a chicken. And since Doug was so much bigger than Ian (and all of the other kids too), Ian was afraid that if he asked Doug to play, Doug would clobber him or smack him hard with a ball, or rock, or his hand, or a stick, or anything he could find. So Ian just avoided Doug and planned on avoiding him for the rest of the school year!

That idea was about to be changed.

"Okay, class," Mrs. Land said. "On Monday we will be changing desks. I've come up with a new seating arrangement. We will change desks every six weeks, so you can all have new neighbors and get to know each other. You will continue to sit with each other at lunch too."

Mrs. Land began naming who would sit where. As Mrs. Land called out more names, Ian's stomach began to flip and flop. She hadn't called his name or Doug's. *Great,* he thought. *I bet I'll have to sit by* Doug! Sure enough, Mrs. Land announced that Ian, Doug, Alan, and Mollie would be together. That meant for lunch too. Ian would be next to Doug all day, except for recess.

Tristan patted Ian on the back and looked at him woefully. "Sorry, Ian," Tristan whispered. Tristan was so glad he didn't have to sit with Doug, but he knew that day was coming.

"Me too," Ian whispered back. "Hopefully we won't be assigned as playmates too."

"Hey," Tristan said as he leaned over to Ian. "Maybe you can make Doug be nice!"

"Yeah, that will happen," Ian replied. "I may as well make arrangements at the hospital, because I know Doug is going to *clobber* me!" Ian looked at Jamie and Ginger and then added, "I guess we had better make the most of today!"

By the time school was out, Ian's stomach felt like it was in his throat, ready to spring out the second he opened his mouth. When Mom and Justin came to pick him up, he practically knocked them down as he rushed through the door. He ran as fast as he could to the car, jerked open the car door, climbed in, and slammed the door shut, hoping to shut out the idea that he would spend the next six weeks at school sitting by Doug.

When Mom got in the car she looked at Ian and said, "What on earth is the matter with you, Ian?" She buckled Justin into his booster seat as Ian told her what horrible events would occur Monday.

"Doug can't be that bad, can he?" Mom asked.

"Oh, yes he can," Ian sobbed. "Remember what he did to that little, brown dog on the first day of school? And he's stolen my turn at the swing, and Ginger's cookies, and Tristan's drink, and cut in front of me in line! He's a big, fat meany! This is the worst day of my life!"

Ian looked at Mom as if she should say, "Right, I forgot about the little, brown dog, and the cookies, juice, and swing! Doug should be locked up in prison. No one is *that* mean!"

"Well," Mom said, "it sounds like maybe Doug just needs a friend. Have you even tried to talk to him, Ian?"

"*No!*" Ian yelled. "He gives me these mean stares and makes a fist every time he sees me looking at him. He looks like he *wants* to beat me to a pulp!"

Justin began giggling and repeated, "Beat me to a pulp!" He giggled some more, unaware of the dangers awaiting Ian on Monday.

"Stop laughing at me, Justin!" Ian screamed. "You don't know how hard it is or how lucky you are!"

"Calm down, Ian!" Mom snapped. "Don't take your anger out on Justin. Just try and be nice to Doug. But, if you ever feel threatened or he tells you he's going to hit you, tell your teacher, okay?"

"Okay, Mom," Ian glumly answered. He had hoped Mom

would tell him she'd talk to Mrs. Land, and he wouldn't have to sit with Doug. But she didn't say that, so Ian began to worry. He worried until Dad got home and promptly told Dad about the tragedy that would befall him on Monday. Dad told Ian to relax and enjoy the weekend.

In spite of his worries and fears, Ian did have a good weekend. It was a busy weekend. On Saturday, he and his family went on a picnic at the zoo. On Sunday after church, Ian and Justin spent the afternoon at Grandy and Pappy's house. Mom and Dad picked them up, and they went to evening services at church. After church, they ate pizza. Ian didn't eat very much, because he was beginning to worry about school. When they went home, it was time for Ian and Justin to get ready for bed.

When Mom and Dad tucked Ian in, he really began to worry. Mom and Dad each prayed that Doug wouldn't clobber Ian.

Then Mom whispered to Ian, "Just be nice to Doug. Maybe you'll find out that he needs a friend." She kissed Ian, turned out the light, and left his room.

Ian stared at the painted Kory. He could hear Justin softly snoring across the hall. Ian rolled onto his back and closed his eyes, hoping so badly that at this very moment Doug's parents had decided to move over the weekend, and he wouldn't have to see Doug. *Fat chance,* he thought. Then he hoped that Mrs. Land would change her mind about moving everyone around. *Fat chance about that too.*

All of a sudden, Ian felt a *thump* on his chest. His eyes jerked open and stared into the face of a leopard. It was Kory!

"I thought you were a dream!" Ian said. He buried his face into Kory's soft fur and hugged him so tightly that Kory's green eyes bulged slightly out of their sockets.

"Nope, I'm not a dream," Kory said. "How about going to my jungle for a while and maybe eating some more buffalo berries?"

"That sounds great!" Ian said. He hadn't eaten much supper because he was so nervous. Now he realized he was hungry.

Kory silently hopped off Ian's bed. Ian climbed onto his back and hung on tightly. He closed his eyes and felt Kory's powerful muscles tighten just before he sprang up to the tree on the wall. When Ian opened his eyes, they were once again in the tallest tree in the jungle.

"Let's go," Kory said. "But hang on! We're going *all* the way down, no stops!" Kory leaped off the branch. Ian ducked his head down by Kory's powerful shoulders and watched branch after branch pass by. It felt like they were flying! After they passed the ninth branch, Kory landed on the ground with a quiet thud.

"Is Exx around?" Ian asked.

"I don't know if you'll see him today," Kory said. "Just before I got you, Exx was slithering up a tree. He had just eaten something and said he needed to rest and digest."

"Oh," Ian said. He didn't want to think about what, or whom, Exx had just eaten, so he abruptly changed the subject. "So, who will I meet today?"

"I don't know," Kory answered. "Let's start walking to the buffalo berry bushes, and we'll see who pops up. That's the thing about the jungle, there's always a surprise or two!" Kory and Ian started walking down the path. Ian listened to the birds squawking and monkeys chattering. Off in the distance, something—maybe a lion or tiger—roared. Kory padded along silently.

"Hey!" Kory said. "I just thought of something you might

like to see. This way!" Kory turned off the path, and he and Ian pushed through bushes until they came to another path. This one was not as well traveled as the other one. Ian walked beside Kory with his left arm on Kory's back. He liked feeling Kory's velvety fur and powerful muscles ripple beneath his hand. Ian wondered what Kory wanted him to see. *Exx digesting his lunch? More buffalo berry bushes? What?* He was just getting ready to ask Kory what he was taking him to see, when two hairy, long-fingered hands wrapped around his head and covered his eyes. Ian began flailing his arms about, then grabbed the hands, which were attached to long, hairy arms, and tried to pry them off his eyes.

"Guess who?" something shouted into Ian's ears.

"Oh, great," Ian heard Kory mumble. Ian managed to pry a couple of fingers off his eyes and whirled around to see to whom they belonged. Through the rest of the squirmy, but strong, fingers, Ian stared into the crossed eyes of a monkey. The monkey was hanging from a tree branch by his long tail and had a banana sticking out of his mouth. The monkey uncrossed his eyes, spit the banana out of his mouth, and grabbed it with his right hand, giving Ian a chance to wrestle free from the other monkey hand.

"You didn't guess who!" the monkey said to Ian.

"How is he supposed to know who you are when he's never met you?" Kory asked the monkey. "This is Ian," Kory said.

"Oh, yeah," the monkey answered. "My name is Mason!" He dropped to the ground and held out his right hand to shake Ian's hand, then realized it was the hand with the banana in it. He shoved the banana into his mouth, and then re-offered his sticky, banana-slimed hand to Ian.

Ian slowly held out his right hand. Mason grabbed Ian's

hand and shook it up and down so fast that Ian felt like it might fall off. Mason smiled at Ian, but his mouth was so full of banana that his cheeks puffed out, and his eyes began to bulge out of his head.

Not wanting to be rude, Ian tried not to laugh at Mason. But Mason looked so funny he couldn't help it. Mason started laughing too, and when he did, pieces of monkey slobber-covered banana flew out of his mouth. Some landed in Ian's hair, some on the ground, and some pieces splattered onto Kory's back.

"*Hey!*" Kory growled at Mason. "I'd rather not wear your lunch!" Mason smiled at Kory, then crossed his eyes, and stuck out his tongue. Ian giggled and wiped the banana out of his hair and then began wiping banana pieces off Kory's fur.

"Is there something we can help you with, Mason?" Kory snarled. "You goofy monkey," he mumbled under his breath.

Mason scratched his head and sidled over to Kory. He grabbed a piece of banana off Kory's fur, held it up, looked at it, and then popped it into his mouth.

How gross, Ian thought.

"No," Mason answered. "I don't need help with anything. I'm just bored, and when I saw you and Ian, I thought I could hang around with you and not be bored!" Mason draped one hairy arm around Ian and the other around Kory and hugged them. "How does that sound?"

Before Kory could answer "Like a nightmare" Ian said, "That sounds great! The more the merrier!"

Kory breathed a heavy sigh and then said, "Very well, but I'll have to take you to the place I was going to take you some other time, Ian."

"Where were you taking him?" Mason asked. "Can I

come?" He began to run his fingers through Ian's hair, looking for bugs (and banana pieces).

"No, you can't come with us to that place," Kory said. "It's a special place, and noisy monkeys aren't invited!"

Mason looked at Ian and whispered, "I think he means me!" Ian giggled, and Mason began screeching. In spite of himself, Kory grinned.

"Well," Ian said, "if we're not going to the special place where noisy monkeys aren't invited, then how about eating some buffalo berries with us?"

"*Buffalo berries!*" Mason shrieked. "I *love* those! Let's go! I'm starving!" Mason bounced up, grabbed a branch, swung up, and scampered off toward the buffalo berry bushes, chattering and shrieking as he went.

Kory sighed. He looked at Ian and said, "Well, I guess we should go to the buffalo berry bushes. But since that silly monkey's gone, it would be a great time to show you the special place I was going to show you!"

"I'd love to see the special place, Kory," Ian said. "But if we don't go to the buffalo berry bushes, we might hurt Mason's feelings."

"True," Kory said. He sighed again and then grinned at Ian. "At least it will be a quiet walk to the buffalo berry bushes!"

Ian laughed and patted Kory's shoulders. "I think Mason's funny," he said.

"You don't see him all of the time," Kory replied.

The leopard and boy turned around and headed back to the main path that would lead them to the buffalo berry bushes. Ian stared in wonder and amazement at the trees and flowers. He heard some elephants trumpeting. They sounded like they were fairly close. Ian hoped he would meet an elephant sometime. When they reached the main path, Ian looked to his left and could see Kory's tree towering over the canopy of the other trees. They turned right, onto the main path, and started toward the buffalo berry bushes.

As they walked they could hear Mason ahead of them, shrieking and chattering as he jumped and swung from tree to tree. Occasionally, a bird would squawk and fly off in a flurry of feathers and leaves. Ian saw a group of monkeys explode from the branches, leaping, whooping, and screeching. Above all of the commotion, Mason could be heard laughing.

"Well, so much for a quiet walk. I can only imagine what Mason did to those creatures," Kory said. Ian grinned at the thought of Mason jumping in the middle of a bird's nest and scaring the poor thing half to death or swinging through a group of unsuspecting monkeys.

"The good thing about Mason being noisy is that there probably won't be any water buffaloes around," Kory said. "Probably not much of anything will be around when they hear that goofy monkey coming," Kory added. Ian snickered and nodded in agreement, hoping he wouldn't run into any water buffaloes. Kory might think Mason was annoying, but Ian could tell that whenever Mason was around, things would definitely not be boring.

As they walked on, the commotions lessened, and then stopped altogether. "Mason must have found the buffalo berry bushes. I bet he's gobbling up buffalo berries," Kory said. "He's only quiet when his mouth is full or he's sleeping. And I *know* he's not sleeping."

"I hope he saves some berries for me," Ian said. "They are *so* good."

"I just hope I don't get buffalo berries splattered on my fur,"

Kory replied. "There's already dried banana on my fur. If we hang around Mason much longer, I'll look like a furry fruit salad!" Ian laughed out loud and patted Kory on the shoulder. Kory purred.

They reached the pool with the silver fish, which had taken one look at Mason and darted beneath some rocks on the other side of the pool. Kory and Ian noticed the fish hovering under the rocks as they walked past the pool to the buffalo berry bushes.

"I don't blame them," Kory whispered to Ian. "I believe I'll do likewise." And with one huge leap, Kory landed on the rock overhanging the pool and buffalo berry bushes.

Mason was indeed at the buffalo berry bushes, cramming berries into his mouth and grabbing more as soon as his hands were free of berries. Since his mouth was overflowing with buffalo berries—and being the greedy monkey that he was—he began making a pile of buffalo berries on the ground next to the pool.

Ian reached down to get a berry off of Mason's pile. Mason stopped chewing, frowned at Ian, and with a muffled yell said, "Ffet moo obn!"

Dropping the berry back onto the pile, Ian walked over to the buffalo berry bushes and began picking berries and eating them. "I *will* get my own!" he said to Mason. "I didn't think you'd mind if I took *one* berry!"

Ian tossed a berry up to Kory, who caught it in his mouth. Ian did this several more times, until Kory announced he had had enough berries. Then Ian ate some berries. Kory purred, and his long tail dangled off the ledge, slowly swaying back and forth like a pendulum on a grandfather clock.

Perhaps, he thought, *I can take Ian to that special place later today*. Kory closed his eyes thinking of what Ian would say when he saw the special place.

Rumble, rumble, crash!

Kory jerked open his eyes and saw a huge water buffalo burst through the bushes, heading straight for the buffalo berry bushes. It was the leader of the group, although the other three water buffaloes were nowhere to be seen. Ian froze in fear, while Mason just kept stuffing his mouth with berries.

Instantly Kory was off the rock ledge. He grabbed Ian's shirt in his mouth, turned swiftly around, and leaped back up on the ledge. He plopped Ian down beside him.

"Thanks!" Ian said, still petrified of the water buffalo. "That was close!"

The water buffalo didn't notice Ian and Kory. He didn't notice Mason either, who was plucking off buffalo berries left and right to keep the water buffalo from getting them. Mason was so busy gathering berries that he forgot about his pile of berries. But the water buffalo spied them and headed straight for them. Just as he reached the pile of berries, Mason froze, remembering his precious stockpile of berries. He watched in horror as the water buffalo began gobbling up the pile of buffalo berries.

"Hey you!" Mason shouted.

The water buffalo raised his head and looked at Mason. His mouth was dripping with purple buffalo berry juice. He glared at Mason, swallowed and said, "My name's not 'you'!"

"Well, whatever it is, you're eating *my* buffalo berries!" Mason shrieked. He appeared to have no fear whatsoever of the water buffalo. His only concern was his pile of berries.

Ian scooted next to Kory and put a hand on Kory's back.

"This is going to be good," Kory whispered to Ian. Ian

nodded as he and Kory watched, barely blinking for fear they'd miss something.

The water buffalo lowered his head, ignoring Mason for the moment, and continued eating the pile of berries. He swallowed again, then looked directly at Mason, and said, "My name is Binky."

"Binky?" Mason said. "*Binky?*" A huge, lumbering, bully of a water buffalo named *Binky?* As Mason thought about this, he began to laugh. He laughed harder. And then he began to hoot and shriek. He jumped up and down and slapped his knees.

Binky took a heavy step forward, squinted his eyes, and snorted. Purple slobbery goo exploded out of his nose. It flew everywhere. A giant glob of slobber flew into Mason's wide-open mouth and slid down his throat. Mason hacked, and coughed, and rolled on the ground. Satisfied with the outcome of his snort, Binky stepped back to what was left of the pile of buffalo berries.

"Heh, heh, heh," he snickered. "Compliments of Binky!"

Mason stopped hacking and rolling on the ground. In an instant, he was on his feet. He zipped over to Binky and stared up at his purple-coated snout. Binky lowered his head and shook his horns menacingly at Mason. Then Binky puckered his lips and made a kissing noise to Mason.

"Here we go!" Kory told Ian as they watched the drama unfold.

"*Aaauugghh!*" Mason shrieked. He had gotten angry when the water buffalo ate his pile of berries and then snorted purple slobber down his throat. But now he was furious! He was not about to be *kissed* by a water buffalo! Quick as a flash, Mason hopped onto Binky's huge head. He grabbed his horns and began shaking Binky's head up and down and back and forth. Then he jumped onto Binky's back and *bit* him squarely between the shoulders! Binky bellowed in pain and began to buck, trying to get rid of the crazy monkey on his back. Mason held on and scampered back to Binky's rear end. He grabbed Binky's tail and pulled it upward and backward as hard as he could! Binky let out a bellow of rage and whipped his head around to knock Mason off his back, but Mason dashed up onto the ledge where Kory and Ian were.

"See you later!" he said as he sped by, jumping to a tree growing by the pool. From there, he swung from tree to tree until he was out of sight.

Binky narrowed his eyes at Kory and Ian and snorted at them. "You had better watch out!" he warned. Then he turned around and rumbled away into the jungle, swishing his tail angrily.

"Wow!" Ian exclaimed. "You were right, Kory. You never know what is going to happen in the jungle! I bet you didn't expect to show me *this* today, did you?"

"Indeed not," Kory said. "I was hoping we wouldn't see any water buffaloes. I'm glad we were in a safe spot! That crazy monkey sure didn't seem to be afraid. *Maybe* next time it will make Binky think before he bullies anyone else. You know, I'm pretty proud of Mason!"

"Me too," Ian agreed. "But I don't know what I'll do if I'm ever face-to-face with Binky or any of the other water buffaloes. I'll probably faint!"

"Well, Mason showed us that we can stand up to them even though they are a lot bigger than we are," Kory said. "I don't know if Binky will tell his buddies what happened to him. He may be too embarrassed, or he may want revenge. Either way, he's going to be as mad as a hornet, so we'll have to be really careful in the jungle. But one of these days, Binky will push someone too far, and he or she won't back down. I just hope I'm there to see it!"

"Maybe it will be you," Ian said proudly. "After all, you are a leopard! You eat these guys!" Ian and Kory laughed.

"Actually, since I hunt alone, I don't eat water buffaloes," Kory answered. "They are probably too tough to chew anyway!" Then Kory looked at Ian and said, "I think you've had enough of the jungle for today. I'll take you home."

"Aren't you going to take me to the special place?" Ian asked. "I really want to see it. Please? Pretty please? Pretty please with sugar on it?" Ian pouted his lips at Kory, hoping his pitiful look would change Kory's mind. It didn't.

"No, that water buffalo is too mad," Kory insisted. "I'll wait until he calms down and isn't terrorizing the jungle. Then I'll take you to the special place. Okay?"

Ian knew he wouldn't win this argument. "Okay," he said glumly. He hopped onto Kory's back and Kory leaped off the ledge. Ian stayed on Kory's back and rode him back to the tree, just in case Binky and his cronies crashed through the jungle at them and they had to jump up into a tree. They saw no signs of any water buffaloes as they made their way back to Kory's tree. Ian could see it before they got there, because it was so much taller than the other trees. It was like a skyscraper.

When they reached the tree, Ian hung on with his arms and legs before Kory could tell him to hang on. Kory leaped from branch to branch until they were at the ninth branch above the ground. Kory lunged toward the tree trunk and landed on the floor of Ian's bedroom. Ian slid off Kory and climbed into bed.

"Sorry for all of the commotion today," Kory said.

"That's okay," Ian yawned. "I enjoyed meeting Mason, and

I like the way he stood up to Binky. Do you think I will ever be that brave?"

"Sure," Kory answered. "Everybody can be brave when they have to be. And just remember, every bully is afraid of *something*. I don't think Binky was afraid of Mason today. Mason just made him mad! Maybe you'll be the one to find out what Binky is afraid of!"

"I hope so," Ian said. "I just hope he doesn't trample me to pieces before I find out! I mean, Binky told us to watch out. He may want to get us! And we didn't do *anything* to him!"

"He won't get you," Kory reassured Ian. "Not while I'm around. How many other boys have their very own leopard to watch out for them?"

Ian smiled. "None," he said.

"Exactly," Kory said. "Now, get some sleep, and I'll come back for you again. Good night, Ian."

"Good night, Kory, and thanks!" Ian was so tired he closed his eyes without looking at Kory. He opened them to smile at Kory, but Kory was gone—back to his jungle, back to the tree on the wall. Ian closed his eyes again and fell asleep.

Dealing with Doug

On Monday morning, Ian woke up before anyone else. He walked into the den and looked at the clock. It was six o'clock. He walked around the corner and down the hall to Mom and Dad's room and peeped in. Mom was asleep, huddled under the covers. Dad was lying on top of the covers, snoring. Ian thought about waking Mom, decided not to, and walked to the kitchen. He saw the chocolate-covered sprinkled donuts Mom had bought yesterday on the way home from church. Ian took a bite of donut, and then remembered why Mom bought the donuts. She had told Ian it would make him feel better about having to sit by Doug for the next few weeks. It didn't. He set the donut on the counter and felt his stomach flip and flop.

"Might as well get dressed," Ian mumbled softly. As he walked to his room, he looked in to see if Justin was awake. He wasn't. Ian walked into his room and opened the closet door, deciding what shirt he wanted to wear. As he looked at his shirts, he got an idea. He walked over to his chest of drawers, opened the third drawer, and pulled out a white shirt made out of silky, slick jersey material. Ian slipped it on and smiled a weak smile. *This shirt will be too slick for Doug to grab*

Ann M. Jayne

me and clobber me, Ian thought. He closed the drawer, then pulled open the drawer below it, and got a pair of navy blue jersey pants. Then Ian put on his socks and shoes. He walked to the bathroom and brushed his teeth and combed his hair. He could hear Justin snoring softly.

Ian walked back to the kitchen. He saw his donut, picked it up, and took another bite. His stomach began flip-flopping again. *Maybe I'll just have some juice,* Ian thought. He opened the refrigerator door and got out the bottle of grape juice. Then he hopped up on the counter and got a glass. He hopped down, unscrewed the lid on the grape juice bottle, and poured some juice into his glass. The grape juice came out so fast his cup nearly overflowed. Ian quickly tilted up the bottle, screwed the lid back on, then placed his lips on the glass and slurped the grape juice down to a safe level.

"Nice save!" Mom said. Ian jumped and spun around.

"You scared me!" he said. Mom put the grape juice back into the refrigerator. She saw the half-eaten donut on the counter.

"Why didn't you eat your donut?" she asked Ian. "You usually wolf those things down in three or four bites!"

"I guess I'm just nervous about school," Ian said glumly. "Do I look like I have a fever? I could stay home today."

"No, you don't look like you have a fever," Mom answered. She felt of his forehead with the back of her hand. "Nope, no fever. You are perfectly healthy, so you can go to school. Is there any reason you don't want to go to school today?" Obviously Mom had forgotten about Ian having to sit by Doug.

Ian rolled his eyes. How could his own mother have forgotten something as important as the imminent doom about to befall her oldest son? "One *big* reason named *Doug!*" Ian

84

quickly reminded Mom. "Didn't you remember that today I have to sit by that big bully for the next six weeks? And with my luck, I bet Mrs. Land changes her mind and decides to make this a permanent seating arrangement!"

"Just be nice to Doug," Mom said as she knelt down on her knees and looked Ian squarely in the eyes. "But if Doug hits you or does anything to hurt you, tell your teacher, or any teacher, immediately!" Mom hugged Ian and then added, "Remember, Ian, that all bullies are afraid of something. Many times they are bullies because they *are* afraid, but they don't want anyone else to know! If you find out what Doug is afraid of or doesn't like, you can beat him. Sometimes, bullies just want attention or to be in control of people. If you ignore Doug or don't do what he says, he'll realize you aren't afraid of him, and he can't control you or intimidate you."

"What does indy—imti—" Ian stammered, trying to say the big word Mom just said.

"Intimidate," Mom answered. "It means to scare someone into doing what you want. That's probably what Doug is trying to do. Not just to you, but to all of the other kids as well. Like I said, bullies are usually afraid or insecure about something. Once you figure out what it is, they won't bother you anymore. They might even become your friend!"

Ian thought about this as he picked up his donut. He finished eating it and drank all of his grape juice before he remembered he was nervous! He watched television, and in a while, Dad was up and dressed, ready to take Ian to school. Mom packed Ian's favorite lunch: a hot dog, barbecue potato chips, grapes, and a bottle of water. As a surprise for Ian, she made chocolate chip cookies last night after he and Justin went to bed. She packed two in the bottom of his lunchbox and wrote a little note for Ian:

Hi Ian! Have a great day! Jesus loves you, and so do I! Love, Mom

Mom added a few *X*s and *O*s for hugs and kisses, then stuck the note on top of the hot dog, and closed Ian's lunchbox.

"Let's roll!" boomed Dad's voice. He kissed Mom and then noticed Justin had gotten up and discovered the chocolate-covered sprinkled donuts. He had no problem eating them. Dad leaned down to kiss Justin on the cheek and noticed the chocolate and sprinkles all over his face. He kissed Justin on the top of his head instead. Ian kissed Mom and followed Dad out the door.

"Don't forget your backpack and lunchbox!" Mom called out to Ian. Ian turned around and grabbed his backpack and lunchbox, kissed Mom again, and slammed the door behind him.

On the way to school, Ian was not very talkative. Usually, he and Dad talked about things or played question and answer games. But not today. Ian was deep in thought and worry.

"What's wrong?" Dad asked. "Didn't you get enough sleep? Or hasn't the sugar from the donut kicked in?" He smiled at Ian, but did not get a smile in return.

"Today's the day I have to start sitting by Doug the bully!" Ian exclaimed. *"For six weeks!"* he added with much emphasis.

"Oh, right," Dad said. "I forgot that started today."

"So did Mom!" Ian cried. He wondered how they *both* forgot that today would be the first day of many days of clobbering for their firstborn son. Ian could understand Justin forgetting about it, but his own Mom and Dad?

"I'm sorry that I forgot," Dad said, "but watch your attitude!"

Ian stared out the window. "I'm sorry too. It's just that I'm so worried about what Doug is going to do to me for the next *six* weeks!" Ian emphasized *six* again in case Dad had already forgotten how long he would have to sit by Doug.

"Well," Dad began, "most of the time you'll be in class. He can't clobber you, even if he wants to, in front of Mrs. Land, now can he? And at recess, don't play with him!"

It was as simple as that. Ian hadn't thought about the fact that Doug couldn't clobber him in class! If he did, that would be a certain trip to the principal's office, and then hopefully, Doug would be expelled from school, and he and his family would have to move to another town to avoid the scandal and embarrassment! Ian began to smile! He was safe! He couldn't get clobbered in class, and he just had to avoid Doug at recess. He'd managed to avoid him so far. He'd just have to do it longer!

By the time Ian got to school, he was feeling better—though still a bit nervous. He wondered what would happen if Doug hit him when Mrs. Land wasn't looking. *There will be lots of witnesses,* Ian thought. Doug hadn't clobbered anybody yet, just threatened them. Ian said a silent prayer that he wouldn't be Doug's first victim. He kissed Dad good-bye, got out of the car, and ran to his room. Mrs. Land was there, but no one else was. Ian hoped Doug was sick today.

"Good morning, Ian!" Mrs. Land beamed and gave him a warm hug. She pointed to his group of desks and told Ian to pick a desk. "Today's the day to switch desks," she said, as if Ian needed to be reminded of that little fact. "Isn't this exciting?"

Nerve racking is more like it, Ian thought. He nodded weakly to Mrs. Land and walked over to his new desk. He put his backpack on the desk closest to Mrs. Land. Then he thought about it and moved his backpack to the opposite desk. Now he was facing Mrs. Land. That way, Doug's back would be to Mrs. Land. If he tried to do anything, Ian could see if Mrs. Land was watching, but Doug couldn't! *What a great idea!*

Just as Ian put his backpack on his desk and sat down, more of his classmates arrived. Alan and Mollie came in at the same time. They came over to their new desks, and Ian laid out the strategy for them. They agreed it was a good idea. Mollie took the desk next to Ian. Allan was across from Mollie and next to Doug. Ian smiled at Mollie. He had totally forgotten she would be sitting by him. That helped ease the pain of sitting with Doug.

The bell rang just as Doug burst into the room. "You're over here, Doug," Mrs. Land told him, pointing to the empty desk across from Ian.

But Doug had another idea. He walked over to Mollie's desk, grabbed her backpack, and then shoved it over to the empty desk. "You're in *my* seat!" he growled to Mollie. Ian and Alan shrank back in their chairs. Mollie stood up, ready to change desks with Doug.

"Sit down at your desk, Doug," Mrs. Land called out. "Class is starting. If you had been here earlier you could have picked out your desk."

Doug clenched his teeth and fists, staring first at Mollie, then Alan, and then finally fixing his gaze on Ian as he walked around to his desk. Mollie leaned across the desk to get her backpack. Doug shoved it so hard at her that it slid across her desk and landed on the floor with a loud thud. Mrs. Land saw what Doug had done, proving Ian's theory that Doug didn't have eyes in the back of his head.

"Was that nice, Doug?" Mrs. Land asked. "You need to pick up Mollie's backpack and apologize to her! We don't treat our friends and classmates that way!"

"Sorry!" Doug grumbled. He stood up and walked behind Mollie, then bent over, picked up her backpack, and handed it to her. He reached out to pull her ponytail, but noticed Mrs. Land was watching. So was the whole class. He sat down in his chair and glared at Ian. Ian quickly took out his reading book and looked up today's lesson. This day was not starting off very well!

Since Doug had gotten in trouble right when school started, he pretty much left everyone alone—until lunch. When they were dismissed for lunch, Ian grabbed his lunchbox and waited for Mrs. Land to dismiss their group. If he was first in line from his group, he could sit between whoever was last in line (that would be Tristan today) and Alan or Mollie. But Ian's group was the last group Mrs. Land called. To make matters worse, Alan and Mollie sprinted to the line before Ian! That meant he would either have to sit across the lunch table from Doug or right next to him.

As soon as they got in the cafeteria, Alan and Mollie made sure they sat by each other. Ian had to sit next to Doug. These would be their lunch seats for the next six weeks.

Great, thought Ian. At least Jamie was across from Ian. He opened his lunch box, read Mom's note, and shoved it in his pocket before Doug saw it. Ian got out his lunch and was pleasantly surprised when he saw the cookies. *Those will sure taste good for dessert,* he thought and then smiled. He set them on the table and began to eat his hot dog and chips. Ian got up to get a napkin. While he was gone, Doug grabbed the two cookies and shoved them in his mouth. He looked at Alan, Mollie, and Jamie, daring them with his eyes to say anything.

When Ian got back to his seat, he didn't notice the cookies were gone. He tried to visit with Alan, Jamie, and Mollie during lunch, but they seemed worried about something. *Maybe they are wishing they had some yummy chocolate chip cookies to eat,* Ian thought. Ian ate the last bite of hot dog, washed it down with a long gulp of water, and got ready for his cookies. *I'll eat the grapes later,* he thought. Ian didn't see his bag of cookies. He looked under his lunch box, then under his chair, and the table, thinking the cookies might have fallen on the floor.

Mollie nudged Alan, and Jamie cleared her throat. Ian looked at Alan and asked, "Alan, do you know what happened to my cookies?"

Alan glanced nervously at Doug, who had a satisfied smile on his face, along with some melted chocolate and crumbs. Alan looked back at Ian and tilted his head toward Doug. Jamie cleared her throat again, rather loudly this time. Mollie just stared at her hands in her lap.

As he turned his head and looked at Doug, Ian saw the remnants of his cookies around Doug's mouth. He noticed the empty plastic baggie and knew what Doug had done.

Doug looked at Ian, then wiped his mouth and patted his stomach. "Mmmmm!" he said. "Delicious!" Then he proceeded to burp one of the loudest burps Ian had ever heard.

"What do you say, Doug?" Mrs. Carter the principal asked. No one had seen her walk up, especially Doug. Before Doug could answer, or not answer as he was planning to do, Mrs. Carter noticed Ian was staring coldly at Doug. "Are you okay,

Ian?" she asked. Ian nodded his head yes. "Did something happen here?" Mrs. Carter asked. She thought something had happened. And she also thought Doug was the reason something had happened, but she couldn't prove it.

"No," Ian said very softly. Mrs. Carter looked at Ian again, then at Doug, and then dismissed their class for recess. Ian couldn't wait to get outside and away from Doug! He practically knocked Jamie down to get to the front of the line.

When they got outside, Alan asked Ian why he didn't tell Mrs. Carter about Doug stealing his cookies. "Because I don't want to be a tattletale!" Ian exclaimed. "And I don't want Doug to beat me up, either! Plus I didn't actually see him take my cookies, so I couldn't really prove that he did it." Ian looked down at the ground, and then added, "Even though he had cookie crumbs and chocolate around his mouth! Doug probably would have lied and told Mrs. Carter that they were his cookies."

"Alan, Jamie and I saw Doug take your cookies and cram them in his mean mouth and eat them!" said Mollie.

"I wanted to tell you," Alan said, "but Doug looked at me like he'd beat me up if I said anything. So I didn't. I'm sorry, Ian."

"It's okay, Alan," Ian said. "They were only cookies. I'm sure we have more at home. Let's go play and enjoy our freedom from Doug! I'll race you to the monkey bars!" Ian took off, and Alan, Mollie, and Jamie ran to keep up. Reed and Tristan were already at the monkey bars. Ian looked around and saw Doug kicking dirt into an anthill. *Better the ants than me,* he thought. Maybe the ants will crawl up his leg, and into his pants, and bite him. The thought of ants in Doug's pants made Ian smile.

After what seemed like an incredibly short time, Mrs. Land blew the whistle for her class to line up and go inside. Ian raced over to her and got right behind her, thwarting any plans Doug might have in store for him on the way inside. Ginger, however, was not so fortunate.

As they were walking toward the school door, Ian heard Ginger yell, "Oh!" Then he heard a thud as she fell onto the sidewalk. Everyone turned around and saw Ginger on her knees, crying. Doug was behind her and did not offer to help her up. Mrs. Land rushed back to help Ginger. Reed and Tristan were already helping her to her feet. She stood up and a thin trickle of blood ran down her leg and soaked into her pink sock.

"What happened, Ginger?" Mrs. Land asked.

Before she could even think about what would happen to her, Ginger blurted out, "Doug stuck his foot out and tripped me!" Fully aware of what she had said, fear began to overtake Ginger. She decided that she wouldn't say anything else, even though she had felt Doug's foot come under her heel. She had also felt his hand push her on her back.

"Is that what happened, Doug?" Mrs. Land asked.

"Maybe it is and maybe it isn't!" Doug replied.

"Well, you can tell Mrs. Carter what did or didn't happen," Mrs. Land said. She led the class into the school, but before they got to their room, she had them wait in the hallway outside Mrs. Carter's office while she took Doug into the office. A few minutes later, she came out of the office, but Doug wasn't with her. No one said a word, but everyone looked into Mrs. Carter's office as they walked by, trying to see what was happening to Doug.

On the way to their room, Mrs. Land let everyone get a drink of water and use the restroom. By the time they got to their room, they were all about to burst with the excitement of Doug being sent to the principal's office. There were many whispers while Mrs. Land put a bandage on Ginger's knee. After Ginger sat down at her desk, the class was still buzzing with whispered questions such as "Why did Doug trip you?" or "Are you okay?" and "Are you scared since you told on him?"

Knowing everyone was excited, Mrs. Land tried to restore order in the room. "Okay, class, let's settle down and work on our spelling words," she said as she began writing their ten spelling words on the chalkboard. As soon as she had finished, the door opened, and Mrs. Carter led Doug into the room. As Doug sat down at his desk, she whispered something to Mrs. Land, and then left the room.

"Your spelling words are written on the chalkboard, Doug," Mrs. Land said as if nothing exciting had happened. "You need to copy them down. When you are finished, we'll go over them."

Ian glanced at Doug. He didn't seem upset at all. No tear streaks or anything. Doug finished writing his words, caught Ian looking at him, and stared back at Ian. Ian looked down at his spelling words. *Same old Doug,* he thought.

Mrs. Land began pronouncing the words and had the class repeat them to her. Ian forgot about Doug and focused on his spelling.

The rest of the afternoon went by quickly. The bell rang and school was out! Ian had survived the first day with Doug. It had cost him two cookies, but that was better than a bloody knee.

Mrs. Carter came in the room and waited while the other kids left. Doug's mother did too. She looked like she had been crying. She was holding a baby wrapped in a pink and yellow blanket. *Poor kid,* thought Ian. *I would hate to have Doug for a big brother!* But before Ian could get too deep in thought about having Doug as an older sibling, Mom and Justin walked in. Ian raced over to the door, ready to leave. "Let's go!" he said, pushing his way through the door between Mom and Justin. On the way home, Ian told Mom and Justin what had happened, from Doug trying to steal Mollie's desk, to stealing his cookies, and finally tripping poor Ginger.

When they got home, Mom let Ian eat two chocolate chip cookies. During supper, he told Dad everything that had happened that day. Mom let him have two more cookies for dessert, and then Ian and Justin went outside to play with the dogs. When the sun began to set, Mom called the boys in. They took their baths and put on their pajamas. It was time for prayers. Ian listened as Mom and Dad thanked God that Ian had been safe at school. Justin thanked God for food (especially cookies) and all the animals (especially tigers). Ian thanked God that Doug hadn't beaten him up, that he wouldn't beat him up tomorrow, and that Ginger's knee would heal. Mom and Dad tucked Justin in and kissed him good night. They tucked Ian in and kissed him too.

Ian stared at the painted Kory. Would he get to go to Kory's jungle tonight? Would he meet Binky again? What would Doug do tomorrow? Ian's eyes grew heavy. Soon all of the questions running through his mind were erased and a soft snoring took their place.

Doug Gets Worse

Since Doug had spent some time in the office with Mrs. Carter, he was somewhat subdued for the next couple of weeks. He didn't bother anyone to the point of them getting hurt, like Ginger, but he did manage to do minor infractions, like hide pencils, or "accidentally" splash someone at the water fountain, or give sullen stares and icy glares if he caught anyone looking at him. But today, he couldn't contain himself any longer.

About an hour before lunch, Mrs. Land passed out a coloring sheet of a scarecrow in a pumpkin patch. Ian was very careful to stay in the lines while he colored. Mrs. Land walked by and complemented Ian on how well he was doing. Ian thought that the scarecrow picture would add a nice touch to the fall and Halloween decorations at home. (Halloween was also Ian's birthday!) As he was coloring, his hand bumped his blue crayon (his favorite color). The crayon rolled across the desk and over to Doug's desk onto Doug's scarecrow paper.

Ian gulped, then politely asked, "Doug, would you please hand me my blue crayon?" Ian held out his hand for the crayon.

"Sure," Doug said slyly. "This crayon?" he asked. Ian nodded. Doug picked up the crayon and snapped it into two pieces. Then he snapped each piece into smaller pieces. He snapped those pieces into smaller pieces. He plopped all of the crayon pieces into Ian's outstretched hand. "There you go, Ian!" he said, adding a cold snicker to it. Ian took the pieces of crayon and looked at Doug. "Well," Doug said. "Aren't you going to say 'thank you'?"

Mollie and Alan looked at each other. Ian noticed Mrs. Land was looking for something in her desk drawer. She hadn't seen anything! He looked at Doug, but said nothing. Ian was very mad. But there was no way he was going to say, "Thank you, Doug. Thank you for breaking my favorite color of crayon into tiny pieces!" He took one of the blue crayon pieces and began coloring the scarecrow's overalls.

Doug stared at Ian. This was clearly not the reaction he was expecting. But he couldn't tell Mrs. Land. How could he explain to her that Ian was being impolite by not thanking him for breaking his crayon into pieces? Doug was mean, but he wasn't stupid! What really bothered him was that Ian hadn't said, "Thank you!"

When it was time for lunch, Alan and Mollie raced to the line. At the lunch table, they whispered to Reed what had happened. Reed passed it on to Ginger, who passed the news on to Tristan. Soon everyone at the table knew what Doug had done to Ian's crayon. But they also knew that Ian had purposely and willfully defied Doug! Ian was a hero. The news spread like a wildfire around the playground, and all of Ian's classmates gathered around him.

"So you aren't afraid of Doug anymore?" Ginger asked Ian. She still had a band-aid on her knee, but had added pink flower stickers to it.

"Of course I'm afraid of him," Ian told her. "But I was so mad at him, I felt like hitting him. I couldn't do that, but I wasn't about to thank him. That's just what he wanted me to do." Ian paused, and then added, "Ginger, when he tripped you, I bet you didn't feel like hopping up and saying 'Thank you, Doug! That really felt good when the concrete scraped the skin off my knee!'"

Ginger giggled at that absurd thought. "No, I didn't feel like saying that to him. But I'm glad you stood up to him." Everyone else nodded their heads in agreement.

"Well, I'm sure Doug isn't happy about what I did," Ian added. They all turned their heads to look at Doug, who was sitting alone under a tree, tossing dirt clods at a beetle. "I'm sure he'll make me pay for it." Ian turned and walked to the monkey bars. His friends followed him, still in a bit of awe about Ian's bravery.

Doug left Ian alone the rest of the day. A few other kids weren't so fortunate. When Doug got up to sharpen his pencil, he pulled Jamie's hair. He "accidentally" kicked Reed's chair when he got up to turn in his penmanship paper. So instead of a nice, neat *M* on Reed's paper, there was an *M* that looked like a jack-o-lantern's mouth. No one said anything though, so Doug was satisfied.

Soon the bell rang, and Ian could forget about Doug for the weekend. And he did. Friday night they went out for pizza. Ian and Justin spent Saturday afternoon in the sand pile. Sunday after church, Ian and Justin played with Rascal and Baloo, and then played basketball in the driveway with Dad. By bedtime, Ian went to sleep without worrying too much about Doug. One week was over!

On Monday morning it was raining. It rained all day, which meant no outside recess. So, Mrs. Land's class stayed inside. She and the other teachers were prepared for indoor recess. There were games, puzzles, and blocks to play with as well as books to read.

Ian and Tristan grabbed the container of blocks and began building a skyscraper. They were almost finished when Doug walked by. He looked at their skyscraper and then started going "Ah … Ah … Achoo!" With the fake sneeze, Doug lunged forward, "accidentally" kicking the skyscraper over. It crashed to the ground and blocks scattered everywhere.

"Bless you, Doug!" Mrs. Land exclaimed as she looked up from her desk. She hadn't seen Doug purposely knock over the skyscraper. She just heard the "sneeze" and saw Doug "fall" into the skyscraper. "I hope you aren't catching a cold from this rain!" Then she saw the blocks everywhere and the stunned, somewhat irritated looks on the faces of Ian and Tristan. "Oh, my," she said. "Ian, Tristan, I'm sorry Doug knocked down your building! I bet he can help you put it back together!"

Ian and Tristan looked at each other in sheer horror.

"Uh," Ian stammered, "we were getting ready to put the blocks up anyway." Tristan nodded his head quickly in agreement. "I'm going to sit at my desk and read," Ian added. He got up and walked to his desk so it wouldn't be a lie.

"Me too!" Tristan hurriedly agreed.

Doug sneered at Ian and Tristan and then sat down to play with the blocks. After a while, Mrs. Land said, "Okay, class, we'll have a bathroom break, then start class. Pick up your toys and line up." Everyone except Doug put away their toys. When they returned from the bathroom, Mrs. Land noticed the blocks were still scattered on the floor. "Doug, you need to put away the blocks," she said.

Doug looked at Mrs. Land, then Ian and Tristan, then back to Mrs. Land. "I didn't get them out," he said matter-of-factly.

"No, but you were the last one who played with them," Mrs. Land reminded him.

"Ian and Tristan got them out and left them on the floor," Doug replied. "I shouldn't have to pick up after them!"

"You played with the blocks after they started reading," Mrs. Land said. "Now, please pick up the blocks so we can start class." She pointed to the blocks and looked at Doug. Her look told him that he wasn't going to win this argument. He stomped over to the blocks, kneeled down on the floor, and began throwing the blocks into the container. When he was finished, he put the container in the cabinet and slammed the cabinet door shut. He shuffled back to his desk and flopped down in the chair, staring icily at Ian. Tristan breathed a sigh of relief that he wasn't sitting with Doug.

It rained all day and all night. It was still raining the next day when Ian got up for school. So during recess, he, Tristan, and Reed drew a town and colored it. "There's nothing Doug can knock down with a fake sneeze," Ian told Tristan and Reed. "We're safe." They were, but Ginger, Jamie, and Mollie weren't. They were playing a board game and Doug walked by, faked another sneeze, and kicked the board, which sent cards and game pieces flying.

Mrs. Land looked up in time to see it happen, but didn't realize Doug had done it on purpose—again. "Bless you, Doug!" she said. "Please help the girls put their game back together." Jamie sighed and Ginger fidgeted. Mollie stared at the ground.

Since Mrs. Land was watching, Doug picked up some cards and a playing piece. When she looked away, he tossed them at Jamie.

"Here!" he hissed and then stomped off. Mollie and Ginger

picked up the rest of the pieces and started the game over, hoping Doug wouldn't come by and "sneeze" again.

By the time school was over, it had stopped raining, and the sun was shining. Ian was glad. They would get to have recess outside tomorrow, and he could get away from Doug. They all could!

The next day at lunch, Ian discovered Mom had made more cookies, because she had packed three with his lunch. Ian ate them first, savoring every morsel and also savoring the fact that Doug didn't get to steal his cookies.

At recess Ian, Reed, Tristan, and Alan headed straight for the sandbox. Since it had rained, the sand was moist and perfect for making sand castles. Soon the boys became consumed with creating a town and forgot all about Doug, who was sitting under a tree, digging up dirt with a stick. Mrs. Land was talking to Miss Denton.

Doug watched the teachers. They were watching the other kids on the playground, but they weren't watching him right now. Occasionally Mrs. Land or Miss Denton would glance at Doug to make sure he hadn't poked out his eye with the stick. Since he hadn't, they would watch the other kids on the playground.

Ian, Reed, Alan, and Tristan were engrossed in making their sand town. Alan and Tristan were smoothing out sand for a street. Ian and Reed were patting wet sand onto the newest building they had made. Five other buildings stood on the sides of the street that Tristan and Alan were making, drying in the warm sun.

"A bee! A bee!" Ian heard Doug shrieking. He looked up just as Doug came crashing through their sand town, running through the buildings, leaving deep footprints on the street.

Sand flew everywhere—in Reed's hair, in Alan's mouth, in Tristan's ears, and in Ian's eyes. Doug kept running wildly from the imaginary bee. Miss Denton ran after him, making sure he didn't get stung, not knowing it was a cruel trick Doug had thought up in order to destroy the sand town.

Ian tried to blink the sand out of his eyes, but it hurt too badly. Mrs. Land came over and told him if he needed to wash out his eyes, he could go inside to the bathroom. Tristan led Ian to the bathroom. Reed and Alan came along too. While Ian rinsed out his eyes, Tristan rinsed out his ears, Alan rinsed out his mouth, and Reed shook the sand out of his hair. By the time the boys finished wiping off the sand, recess was over. Ian's eyes were red, and irritated, and burning. As they walked back to their room, Ian wondered if he would go blind. *What a horrible day this has been,* Ian thought. Doug looked at Ian and grinned a sly grin.

Ian was so angry at Doug. And he just couldn't believe Mrs. Land and Miss Denton thought a bee was really after Doug. That made him mad too. *I wish it had been a bee,* Ian thought. *And I wish it had really stung Doug! Stung him on his stupid, ugly face!* He knew he shouldn't wish pain on anyone. But his eyes hurt. And they were filling up with angry tears, which made them sting even more.

Doug saw Ian's eyes filling up with tears. He leaned across his desk and said, "What's the matter, Ian? Are you gonna cry because your sand castle got stepped on? Boo-hoo-hoo!"

"Mrs. Land!" Ian shouted as suddenly as he could. Doug shrank back in his chair. Surely Ian didn't have the guts to tell on him! He had the perfect excuse. He was being chased by a bee. Ian didn't know there wasn't a bee, Doug reasoned with himself. He swallowed hard and began rummaging through his desk, getting out his pencil.

"Yes, Ian?" Mrs. Land walked over to Ian and put her hand on his shoulder.

"My eyes are really hurting," Ian said.

Mrs. Land looked at Ian's eyes. They were really red. "I can certainly see why they would hurt. I think they might still have sand in them," she said.

Ian nodded. "My mom may need to take me to the eye doctor. May I go call her and have her pick me up?"

"Yes you may," Mrs. Land said. "I certainly hope your eyeballs aren't scratched!"

Ian hadn't thought of that. "Me, too," he said, looking at Doug. Ian grabbed his backpack and left to call Mom. *I hope I can find the office before I go totally blind,* he thought.

When Mom arrived, Ian told her what had happened. "And I *don't* think a bee was chasing Doug!" he said.

"Well, that will be hard to prove," Mom said. "But on the way over here, I made an appointment with your eye doctor. We'll see what he says about your eyes. I bet they are just irritated."

Irritated like me, Ian thought. *Now I get to go to the doctor, and he'll probably put those drops in my eyes that really sting! That's just great! All because of Doug the bully.*

The doctor did not have to put the stinging drops in Ian's eyes. He said Ian's eyes weren't scratched, and he wouldn't go blind either. But he did tell Ian to rest and keep a cool washcloth on his eyes for the rest of the day. The doctor told Mom that if Ian's eyes felt worse or got redder to call him at once.

At home, Ian lay on the couch with the cold cloth over his eyes, listening to the cartoons Justin was watching. His eyes were feeling better, but he was still so angry. He couldn't stop thinking about Doug or wondering how Mrs. Land couldn't see what was happening. *Why is Doug so mean? How can Mrs. Land not realize that Doug is doing these things on purpose? Did she miss "How to Handle Bullies" in college?*

When Dad got home, Ian told Dad *everything* that had happened. Dad checked Ian's eyes and verified the eye doctor's diagnosis that Ian would not go blind. Then he gave Ian a hug and kiss.

"I'll have a talk with Mrs. Land," Mom said. "You have to remember, Ian, she has sixteen kids to watch, plus the others on the playground. She wouldn't ignore something Doug has done. She probably didn't see what he did, or truly believed he really sneezed or was being chased by a bee. But I'll talk to her, just so she's aware of what Doug's doing. Maybe she'll watch him a little closer."

Ian finished supper and went to take a bath without being told. After his bath, he put on his pajamas, brushed his teeth, and then crawled into bed. Mom and Dad came in to tuck him in and say prayers.

"I promise I'll talk to Mrs. Land," Mom whispered to Ian.

"Thanks," Ian sighed. "I'm just afraid someone's really going to get hurt by Doug. And I *don't* want it to be *me!*"

"Me neither," Mom said. "Now go to sleep. I love you!" Mom leaned down and kissed Ian's eyes to make them get better faster.

"I love you too, Mom," Ian said. After Mom left to tuck Justin in, Ian stared at the painted Kory, then rolled onto his back, and closed his eyes, wondering what Doug would do tomorrow.

The Special Place

Thump!

Ian opened his eyes and saw Kory staring at him. "Hello, Ian," Kory purred.

"Hello, Kory!" Ian replied. "Do I get to go to your jungle tonight?"

"Sure, if you want to," Kory said. "Or you can stay here and sleep."

"No way!" Ian said, throwing back the covers and climbing onto Kory's back. "I need to go to your jungle. I had a tough day at school. I'm ready for some fun!"

"Let's go then!" Kory said, and waited until he felt Ian hang on. Then he lunged through the tree on the wall and into his jungle, landing on the top branch of the tallest tree in the jungle. Not wanting to waste any time, Kory leaped toward the ground, gliding silently past nine branches until his huge paws landed quietly on the ground.

"Are we going to the special place?" Ian asked.

"Why not?" Kory said. "I haven't seen Binky or any of his buddies lately. This way, Ian." Kory turned to his left and began walking down an overgrown jungle path.

"Don't we need to go on the main path until it forks into

the other path?" Ian remembered that was the way they went last time. That's where they had met Mason.

"This way is a shortcut," Kory said. "I want you to have as much time as possible in the special place. And I don't think Mason will be in this area of the jungle," he added. Ian grinned, remembering how goofy and greedy Mason had been.

They began walking down a path Ian had never seen before. It seemed darker, almost creepy. *I bet there are some big, old snakes around here,* Ian thought. *It might be a good place for Binky to hide and wait.* He moved closer to Kory and kept his left hand on Kory's back.

"What's wrong?" Kory asked. "You look worried, and you're unusually quiet."

"I was just thinking about what would happen if Binky charged through the bushes at us!" Ian said.

"Don't worry about that," Kory answered. "He usually doesn't get too far from the buffalo berry bushes, although there might be a few buffalo berry bushes around here. But I wouldn't be too concerned about him sneaking up on us. He's pretty noisy. I think we could hear him coming." Kory looked at Ian reassuringly and then said, "Watch your step, Ian."

Ian looked up in time to see a crystal clear stream. Kory bounded over the stream. Ian waded across, feeling the cool water rush around his feet and into his shoes and socks. He bent down and splashed some water in his eyes—even though they no longer hurt. *How am I going to explain how I got all wet to Mom,* he wondered.

But he forgot about that when Kory said quietly, "We're almost there. You need to be very, very quiet. No talking or stepping on twigs. And once we get to the special place, you need to be very still until I say it is okay."

"Is the special place dangerous?" Ian asked, clutching Kory a little tighter and listening to his shoes squish as he walked along. He hoped they weren't making too much noise. He also noticed the jungle around the path was getting darker and denser. It looked like this path was not traveled on very often.

"Of course not!" Kory answered. "If it was, I wouldn't even think of bringing you to it! You just won't understand why it's so important to be still and quiet until we get there. Okay?"

"Whatever you say, Kory," Ian said. "I trust you." He felt better knowing Kory wouldn't purposely put him in danger. And his shoes had stopped squishing.

"Good," Kory whispered. "Now, we're just about there so be very, very quiet." Ian nodded and made the motion of zipping his lips. He let Kory lead since Kory could see better in the dimly lit jungle. Ian held onto Kory's tail and followed him as quietly as he could. Kory crept along quietly and then stopped. He motioned for Ian to come up by him. Ian obeyed and noticed the path stopped and seemed to be swallowed up by thick, green bushes. They were so thick Ian couldn't even see through them. "As quietly as you can, peer through the bushes," Kory whispered.

Ian nodded and gently put his hands on some branches. Gingerly and quietly, he moved the branches apart. A small ray of sunlight peeped through, and a pale pink butterfly flitted by.

"Go ahead," Kory whispered. "Open the bushes a little more." Ian nodded, stepped forward, and pushed the branches open even more. More sunlight beamed through, and a few more butterflies flitted by. Ian took another few steps, pushing away more branches. Suddenly, rays of sunlight burst through the bushes. When Ian's eyes adjusted to the bright light, all he

could do was stare at what was on the other side of the bushes. It was truly amazing.

There were hundreds, no *thousands* of butterflies flying around in a huge meadow filled with wildflowers. There were large flowers growing on tall stems and tiny flowers growing in clusters on the ground. Some had long petals, and some had short petals. The flowers were bright and colorful, like a rainbow. So were the butterflies. There were pink, green, yellow, orange, and lavender butterflies. Some were even black or dark purple and reflected the light so that they reminded Ian of Mom's opal ring. Some butterflies had colorful spots or stripes. Ian watched in wild-eyed wonder as butterflies silently flew here and there. As he watched them, he noticed that across the meadow there was a beautiful lake. The lake sparkled like a million diamonds. Beyond the lake and around the meadow was the jungle. Ian thought that this place was like a circle cut out of the jungle, then filled in with wild flowers, colorful butterflies, and a shimmering lake. This was the most beautiful place he had ever seen. He couldn't have ever dreamed of a place like this. *This must be what heaven looks like,* Ian thought.

"Okay, Ian," Kory whispered, "step very slowly and quietly through the bushes. Then stand very, very still." Ian nodded, not wanting to take the chance of answering Kory and have the butterflies fly away. Slowly he pushed the bushes farther apart and stepped through them. He held them open and Kory stepped through silently. They stood as still as statues on the edge of the meadow.

In a few minutes, several butterflies flew over to Ian. A green one landed on his head and several purple ones fluttered around his face. A few pink and yellow butterflies lit on Ian's shoulders and slowly moved their wings back and forth. Ian barely breathed. A large, black butterfly landed on Ian's chest. It was as big as his hand. The sunlight reflected pink, and purple, and yellow hues on the butterfly's wings. Ian watched the butterfly move up and down as he breathed. It twitched its wings like it might fly away, but then folded them back and rested on Ian's chest.

"Follow me, but walk very, very slowly," Kory whispered to Ian. Kory and Ian began walking ever so slowly toward the middle of the meadow. A couple of pink butterflies flitted off, but the rest stayed on Ian, hitching a ride to wherever Ian was going. Several blue butterflies landed on Kory's back. They rode on him as he crept out into the meadow. Ian and Kory walked carefully through the flowers, trying not to disturb the butterflies. Some flew up and scattered, but most of them stayed on the flowers, sucking up the sweet nectar.

When Ian and Kory reached the middle of the meadow, Kory told Ian to stand still and see what would happen. Ian stood as still as a stone. Several more butterflies flew up to him and started to land on him, but when they realized he wasn't a flower, they flew off. But many other butterflies did fly by and land on Ian. In a few minutes, Ian was covered from his head to his belly button in butterflies! He glanced over and saw that Kory was covered in butterflies too. Kory slowly raised his long tail into the air and butterflies swarmed to it, landing on it and lining up like birds on a wire.

A tiny, pink butterfly flitted around Ian's head and landed on his nose. It stuck out its tiny proboscis and searched for nectar. That really tickled, and Ian twitched his mouth back and forth, not wanting to move and scare it or the other butterflies away. Slowly he raised his right arm and moved his hand toward his nose. All of the butterflies on his arm stayed on his arm. Ian wiped at his nose and the tiny, pink butterfly flew up to his head.

"*Achoo!*" Ian sneezed so suddenly that he didn't even know he was going to sneeze. At once the butterflies flew frantically off Ian. But after his sneeze, they grouped together like a school of fish, turned in unison, then flew back to Ian and landed on him again. The way they all moved together was so cool that it gave Ian an idea.

"Whooo!" Ian yelled. He didn't yell too loudly, but it wasn't a whisper either. Again the butterflies took off, but as suddenly as they flew off Ian, they regrouped and landed on him again.

"I think it's safe to say they approve of you, Ian," Kory purred. With that, he roared, and the butterflies flew off him and Ian, formed one huge group, then split back up again, landing back on the leopard and the boy.

Ian raised both of his arms. The butterflies lifted their wings, but didn't fly away. He lowered his arms and watched them flutter in the breeze his arms made. "This is fun!" he exclaimed.

Kory and Ian began walking through the meadow. They were still covered in butterflies, but as they walked through the flowers, the butterflies on the flowers would fly around. Ian began waving his arms, and Kory swished his tail. The butterflies on them flew up and mingled with the other butterflies flying around. Then they would settle back onto the leopard or boy. It was the coolest thing Ian had ever seen, like confetti falling from the sky.

Ian continued playing with the butterflies until they grew tired of flying around. "I think they're getting tired," Kory said.

"I'm sort of tired too," Ian yawned. A tiny, orange butterfly flew into Ian's open mouth. Ian coughed, not wanting to swallow it. His breath blew it away unharmed.

"I guess it's time to go then," Kory said. He turned around and headed for the edge of the meadow. Ian followed him. The butterflies were still hitchhiking, but when Ian and Kory reached the bushes at the edge of the meadow, the butterflies exploded off them and flew back to the flowers. Looking back at the meadow before he stepped into the darkness of the jungle, Ian noticed how different the meadow looked. It was still bright and colorful, but now it was also peaceful and calm. All of the butterflies were resting or drinking nectar.

"Good-bye," Ian yelled and waved to the butterflies. In unison they all flapped their wings a few times, and then grew still again.

"I believe they like you," Kory purred. He was glad he had brought Ian here. What a perfect time they had had. He and Ian began walking back to his tree.

"My brother Justin has got to see this place!" Ian exclaimed. "Do you think he can come to the jungle with us sometime?"

"I don't see why not," Kory answered. "But he'll have to ride on someone else. I can't carry both of you."

"Maybe Binky will give him a ride!" Ian joked.

"Yeah, right!" Kory laughed.

As they walked back, Ian noticed the trail was muddy and slippery. "Did it rain?" he asked Kory.

"Looks like it," Kory said. "It rains a lot in the jungle. It is a rainforest after all."

All of a sudden, the ground began to shake. The leaves on the bushes and ferns and trees jiggled and shimmied. Ian saw a few mice zip in front of him and hide under a bush. He heard a sound like thunder—only it didn't stop. Whatever the sound was, it was getting louder. And closer. Then Ian heard snorting. Before he or Kory could leap aside, Binky and his three buddies came galloping down the path toward them.

Ian froze in fear. Kory grabbed Ian's shirt and jerked him to the side of the path. Binky and the other water buffaloes kept on charging, racing past where Ian and Kory had just stood on the path. As they thundered by, giant clumps of mud splashed onto Ian and Kory. They kept getting pelted with mud until the last water buffalo passed by.

Ian wiped mud off his face and out of his eyes, just in time to see Binky whirl around and charge back toward him. Just as Binky reached Ian and Kory, he came to a sliding stop and snorted.

"This is your second warning!" he bellowed. "The next time you two won't be so lucky! You'll wish the only thing that happened to you was getting mud on you!" He snorted again and stomped his left front foot, sending one last splash of mud onto Ian and Kory. Then he and his buddies tromped off into the jungle. A glob of mud was about to fall into Kory's right eye, but Ian wiped it off with a shaky hand.

"It's okay, Ian," Kory said. "They're gone. But to be safe, hop on my back until we get to my tree." Ian didn't argue and wasted no time climbing onto Kory's back. It began to rain on the way back to the tree. By the time they reached the tree, they were soaked to the skin, but all of the mud had been washed off.

"Hold on," Kory instructed Ian. Ian held on super tight since his legs and Kory's fur were wet. Kory leaped up one branch at a time, being very careful in case the branches were slick.

"Thanks so much for showing me the special place. I've

never seen anything like it. It was absolutely beautiful!" Ian said as he stroked Kory's wet fur.

"I always enjoy going there," Kory replied. "Those butterflies really liked you. We'll have to go back. I'm just sorry Binky had to ruin a perfect trip to the jungle for you."

"It's not your fault," Ian said. "I just wish he wasn't mad at us. We didn't do anything to him. Mason did, but only because Binky provoked him."

"That's the thing about bullies, though," Kory added. "I think Binky was really embarrassed, so to act tough, he had to threaten us. If it makes you feel any better, I haven't seen Mason since the incident. Maybe he's smarter than I thought!" Ian giggled and hugged Kory.

"Now hang on one more time," Kory said. Kory sprang toward the trunk of the tree and landed in Ian's room. Ian was back in his pajamas, and dry. He slid off Kory's back and hugged him again. He could hear Justin snoring.

"Maybe Justin can go with us to the jungle next time," Ian said.

"That's fine, Ian," Kory said, "but remember he'll have to have a buddy to bring him. Two boys won't fit on my back."

"Maybe he'll find one," he said, climbing into bed. "Thanks for a great time, Kory." He closed his eyes and smiled.

"You're welcome, Ian," Kory whispered. He heard footsteps coming down the hall and leaped into his tree.

Mom looked in Justin's room and smiled, listening to him snore. Then she peeped into Ian's room and saw him snuggled under his covers. She looked at the leopard on the wall. For a moment, she thought it looked like it was looking back at her.

"Boy I'm tired," she whispered to herself. She turned around

Kory's Jungle

and walked back down the hall to her bedroom, not realizing the leopard *was* watching her as she left her son's room.

The Perfect Pumpkin

It was Saturday. In one week, it would be Halloween and Ian's tenth birthday! He and Mom were going shopping for his party decorations and cake. Justin was staying home with Dad. They were going to wash the car.

Ian couldn't wait for his party. It was going to be so much fun. He was going to have a trick-or-treat party! He had thought of the idea all by himself. His friends would come over for hot dogs and cake, wearing their Halloween costumes of course, and then they would all go trick-or-treating. Ian invited Jamie, Reed, Tristan, Alan, Ginger, Mollie and another boy named Jackson. He was *not* inviting Doug, as if Mom had to ask him that. He and Mom had made the invitations out of orange paper and Halloween stickers three days ago and mailed them to his friends.

"This sounds like it is going to be a fun party, Ian," Mom said as she drove them to the party supply store.

"Don't buy scary decorations," Ian informed Mom. "Justin or some of my friends might get scared if the house is too scary."

"Right, no scary decorations," Mom noted. She smiled, knowing Ian didn't like scary decorations any more than Justin did. She didn't like scary decorations, either!

When they got to the party supply store, they were amazed at the amount of Halloween decorations. Some were really, really scary. Mom and Ian went to another aisle and found some fun decorations. Mom got some orange and purple lights for the windows. She also got some fake spider webs with plastic spiders in them. Ian picked out window decorations with owls, bats, and black cats on them. They got glow-in-the-dark eyes to put in dark corners and under the couch. And for the punch, Mom got a plastic cauldron with a skeleton hand ladle. Ian picked out paper plates, napkins, and cups with black cats and pumpkins on them. Mom got some orange plastic forks and a black plastic tablecloth. Their cart was full, so Mom paid for everything, and then she and Ian went to the bakery to pick out his cake.

Ian found a cake decorated just like he wanted. It had purple icing with a black cat and bats, a big yellow moon and orange pumpkins made out of icing. He also wanted his cake to be chocolate *and* vanilla. The lady that worked at the bakery said she could make the cake half chocolate and half vanilla. She said she would write "Happy Birthday, Ian" on the moon. It would be ready the following Saturday by 5:00, just before the party.

Mom and Ian went home and unloaded the party decorations. Since it was nearly lunchtime, Dad decided they should go to their favorite hamburger restaurant for lunch before picking out pumpkins. Justin and Ian raced to the car.

"Beat ya!" Justin exclaimed as Dad and Mom walked calmly to the car.

"You're faster than me," Dad said. Everyone got in, and Dad drove to the restaurant. The boys were so excited about getting pumpkins that they gobbled up their hamburgers.

"Let's go!" Ian said.

Mom looked at Ian and said, "Dad and I aren't finished with our hamburgers yet. We prefer to *chew* our food." Ian and Justin giggled, and then finished their curly fries. It seemed like an eternity before Mom and Dad finished their food.

Finally, Dad said, "Let's go!" The boys grabbed Mom and Dad's hands since they had to cross the parking lot, but walked as fast as they could. They talked about the kinds of pumpkins they wanted to get as Dad drove to the pumpkin patch. Justin wanted one so big he could get inside it. Dad told him that was out of the question, because he was not going to clean out a pumpkin that big, and he didn't want Justin smelling like a pumpkin! Ian didn't know how big of a pumpkin he wanted. He just knew he had to find the *perfect* pumpkin.

When they got to the pumpkin patch, Ian couldn't believe how many pumpkins there were. It looked like an ocean of pumpkins! There were orange pumpkins, white pumpkins and greenish-orange pumpkins, big pumpkins, little pumpkins, fat pumpkins, thin pumpkins, round pumpkins, short pumpkins, and tall pumpkins. Ian saw some pretty odd-looking gourds too. And picking out pumpkins wasn't the only thing to do at the pumpkin patch. There were ponies to ride, a hay bale maze, a hayride, and a petting zoo.

"I want to ride a pony!" Justin yelled and sprinted off toward a fat, brown pony.

"Hold it!" Dad said, grabbing Justin's shirt. "Let's get your pumpkins first before someone else gets the ones you want. Then you boys can ride the ponies and play."

"You and Mom have to get pumpkins too," Ian said. Then he raced off to look for his perfect pumpkin. Ian didn't bother looking at the tall pumpkins or greenish-orange pumpkins. His pumpkin would be like ones in pictures, a brilliant orange with a stem on top and as round as a basketball.

Justin spied a patch of large pumpkins and climbed on top of a really big one. He yelled at Dad that this was the one he wanted. Dad walked over to it and saw the how much the pumpkin cost.

"This pumpkin costs more than your shoes, Justin!" he said. "If you can carry this pumpkin, I'll get it for you. If you can't, then you better pick out a pumpkin that you can carry."

Justin slid off the pumpkin and tried to lift it. His arms wouldn't even reach all the way around it. "Will you help me carry it, Dad?" Justin asked hopefully. Dad shook his head no. Justin kept trying to lift the pumpkin (which weighed more than he did) until he began to sweat. Finally he gave up and went to look for a pumpkin he could carry.

Meanwhile, Ian was still searching for the perfect pumpkin. Every time he thought he had found it, he'd discover that it had a rotten spot on it, or a mouse had chewed around on it, or the stem was broken off, or it had big green spots on it. He was just about to give up, when he heard a meow. He looked around and saw a beautiful, yellow cat sitting on a pumpkin. The cat hopped off the pumpkin and began rubbing around Ian's legs, purring as loudly as it could. Ian reached down to pet the cat and noticed the pumpkin it had been sitting on. It was bright orange, like a sunset, and almost as round as a basketball. Ian grabbed the curly stem and turned the pumpkin around. He didn't see any spots, or blemishes, or chew marks on it. He had found his perfect pumpkin!

It was a little bit heavier than he thought it would be, but he grunted, and groaned, and finally picked it up. The cat was still winding around his legs, and he almost fell down. Ian scooted the cat away with his foot, but it happily followed him over to Dad.

"Here's my perfect pumpkin," Ian said.

"It is a nice pumpkin, Ian," Dad said. "Justin found his pumpkin, and Mom is getting some gourds."

Justin's pumpkin was greenish-orange. The green and orange blended together in almost a striped pattern. Justin loved tigers and decided the "tiger pumpkin" was the one for him. It was thinner than most of the pumpkins and taller too. It was a good-sized pumpkin, but not big enough for him to get inside.

"Aren't you getting a pumpkin?" Ian asked Dad.

"Oh yeah, I forgot!" Dad said. He walked over to a pile of pumpkins, grabbed a short, fat, white one, then brought it back and placed it with the others.

"That didn't take long," Ian said.

"No," Dad said, "because two little boys already picked out the two best pumpkins. I had to settle for second best!"

While Dad paid for the pumpkins, Mom took the boys over to the ponies. They had to wait because other kids were riding them. But that gave them time to decide which pony they wanted to ride. Ian decided he liked a dapple-gray pony and Justin still wanted to ride the brown pony he had seen earlier.

When the other kids got off the ponies, Ian walked over to the gray pony. A man named Bart helped Ian on the pony.

"This is Harry," he said. Ian patted Harry's neck. Bart helped Justin onto the fat, brown pony. "And this is Luke," he said to Justin. A teenage girl named Hannah came over to lead Luke around the corral while Bart led Harry around. Justin noticed a black and white spotted pony standing at the hitching post. He asked Hannah who that was.

"That's Jingles," she said. "Would you like to ride him next?"

"Yeah!" Justin said.

Hannah led Luke around the corral several more times, then stopped him and helped Justin get down. She tied Luke up, then untied Jingles and helped Justin up on Jingles. As she began leading Jingles around, Bart asked Ian if he wanted to ride a different pony.

"No thanks," Ian said. "I like Harry. I'll keep riding him." So Bart led Harry and Ian around until more kids showed up to ride. Ian climbed off Harry and hugged his neck. "Thanks, Harry," he whispered. Justin patted Jingles and Luke, and then the boys walked out of the corral and met Mom and Dad.

"Was that fun?" Mom asked. "It looked fun. Too bad I'm too big to ride the ponies."

"It was fun!" Ian said and began telling her all about Harry and what a nice pony he was. Justin told Dad about Luke and Jingles. Then both boys saw the hay bale maze and raced off to get in it. They ran and played and climbed until they were red and sweaty.

"You boys need a cold drink," Dad said. He bought a couple of bottles of soda for them. "This would have been a good place for your party, Ian," Dad said.

Ian gulped down some soda and nodded his head. "Maybe next year," he said. "I want to have a trick-or-treat party this year!"

"That will be fun too," Dad added. "Not too many kids

are born on Halloween, so your party will be different from everyone else's!"

"Let's go on the hayride," Mom said. "I hear the tractor coming." They hurried over and were first in line. The tractor pulling the hay wagon sputtered its way up a little hill and then chugged over to where everyone was waiting to ride. Ian and Justin climbed onto the trailer and walked up to the front nearest the tractor. They plopped down in the hay and Mom and Dad sat on hay bales behind them. When everyone was on, the tractor jerked to a start and chugged off, with the trailer bouncing along behind it.

After the hayride, Ian and Justin petted and fed the baby goats and lambs at the petting zoo. Ian got butted by a very hungry and impatient goat. Goats suddenly became his least favorite animal, and Ian decided he had had enough of the petting zoo. He and Justin rode Harry and Jingles one more time and then it was time to go home. It was almost dark when they got home. While Mom fixed spaghetti, the boys took baths to wash off the barnyard dirt.

During supper, Dad asked the boys what they wanted to be for Halloween. Neither boy knew what he wanted to be.

"Well, how about fairy princesses or ballerinas?" Dad asked.

"*No!*" both boys exclaimed at once.

Justin began to think while he ate his spaghetti. As he swallowed an unusually large bite, he got an idea. "I'm going to be a pirate," he said slyly. "And I want to wear *two* eye patches!"

"Don't be ridiculous, Justin!" Ian scolded. "You wouldn't be able to *see!*"

"Well, I could poke little holes in them," Justin said.

"One eye patch will be plenty," Mom told Justin. "We saw some pirate costumes at the party supply store. Tomorrow after church we can get your costume. Maybe you'll see a costume you like, Ian."

Ian still didn't know what he wanted to be, but he knew he was *not* going to be a fairy princess or ballerina. Or a pirate with two eye patches. Maybe he'd be a policeman or a doctor. He looked around the room and saw Kory lying on the couch.

"I've got it!" Ian said. "I want to be a leopard!"

"A leopard?" Mom asked.

"Yes, a golden yellow leopard with black spots," Ian said. "That's what I want to be for Halloween."

"A black panther would be easier," Mom said.

"But Kory's not black," Ian said. "I want to look like him, with ears and whiskers and a tail!"

"Well, you can look for your leopard costume at the party supply store tomorrow, Ian," Mom said. "And we'll need to get the ingredients to make sugar cookies. I thought it would be nice if you took cookies to school for your birthday. We can make the cookies Thursday night for your party on Friday. How does that sound?"

"Great!" Ian said. He was so excited about his trick-or-treat party, and now he was going to have another party at school! He hoped Doug would be sick on Friday so that they could really have a fun class party.

Justin yawned. He was full and tired.

"I think it's time for two boys to go to bed," Dad said. "You've had a busy day! Go brush your teeth, and then we'll say prayers."

After the prayers, Mom went into the den and called Grandy. She told her what Ian wanted to be for Halloween.

"I can buy some material and a pattern tomorrow and

make it for him," Grandy said. "I'll try to have it ready by Wednesday."

"Thanks," Mom said. "I'll talk to you tomorrow night to see what you found."

So the next day after church, Dad stopped at the party supply store. Justin found his pirate outfit, complete with a hook for his hand and a parrot for his shoulder. He even found a plastic pirate sword and revolver. Ian looked for a leopard costume but didn't find one.

"We'll find one," Mom told him.

"But Halloween is Saturday!" Ian said. "What if we don't find one?"

"We'll find a leopard costume, Ian. I promise!" Mom said. That night after the boys were in bed, Mom called Grandy to see if she had had any luck.

"I'm cutting out the material right now," Grandy said.

"Ian will really be surprised," Mom said.

"That's what grandmothers are for," Grandy said.

"Yes, but when Ian and Justin have kids, they better hope the other grandmother can sew!" Mom replied.

"I'll call you when I finish it," Grandy said. "Then you can bring Ian over, and he can try it on."

"Thanks again," Mom said. She went to bed smiling, knowing that Ian would be totally surprised about his costume.

The Perfect Costume

On Wednesday, Mom's cell phone rang. It was Grandy and she had finished Ian's costume. "I'm on my way to get Ian from school," Mom said. "We'll be over in a little while. You certainly got it done quickly!"

"I worked on it all day," Grandy said. "Then if I need to make any adjustments, I'll have time before Ian's party."

"Thanks a lot, Mama," Mom said. "We'll see you in a while!"

When Justin and Mom got to school, Mom told Justin she had to talk to Mrs. Land. He and Ian would have to wait in the hall.

"Can I bring my pirate sword in?" Justin asked.

"Yes, but don't stab anyone with it or slice them open!" Mom cautioned Justin.

"Arghh, I won't," Justin said. "But ye take all the fun out of being a pirate!"

When Mom and Justin walked into Ian's room, Reed saw Justin's pirate sword and made a beeline over to see it. But Reed's mother suddenly appeared in the doorway, and he was very reluctant to leave. Other parents came, and soon all of the kids were gone. Mom told Ian and Justin to wait in the hall. Much to Ian's dismay, Mrs. Land closed the door! Now he couldn't hear what they were saying!

"Mrs. Land, Ian has some concerns about Doug," Mom began. "He doesn't think the things that Doug does are accidents, like the bee and sneezing. He's really afraid Doug is going to hurt him or someone else."

"I can tell Doug has some anger problems," Mrs. Land said. "But I didn't ever think he would deliberately do something harmful to anyone. I don't want anyone to get hurt. I will watch him more closely. And I will tell the other teachers to watch him carefully when they have recess duty."

"That makes me feel better," Mom said. "And I know Ian will feel better. He really dreads coming to school since he has to sit by Doug."

"Ian is such a good student," Mrs. Land said. "I hate to think he dreads coming to school. I'll watch their group more closely. And we'll be changing groups in a few weeks, too. I'll make sure Doug doesn't get in the same group with Ian."

"Thank you, Mrs. Land," Mom said. "I just wanted you to be aware of the situation. I'm sure everything will get better. Good-bye."

"Good-bye," Mrs. Land replied as she walked out the door with Mom.

"Good-bye, Mrs. Land," both boys said together. Mrs. Land winked at Ian, and he felt better at once. He still couldn't wait to get in the car and ask Mom what they had talked about. In fact, Mom had barely sat down in the car when Ian asked her what had happened.

"She said she'd watch Doug closer and tell the other teachers to watch him closer too," Mom answered.

"That's it?" Ian asked incredulously. "She isn't going to try to have Doug expelled?"

"For what, Ian? She can't prove he *deliberately* did those things. But now she is aware of what he's doing, so she'll watch him more closely." Mom smiled at Ian. "Just relax. Mrs. Land *and* the other teachers will watch Doug more closely, and he won't know it. And Mrs. Land said in a few weeks you will be changing desks, and she promised she won't put you in the same group as Doug. Now, just think about your birthday party, and let's go find your costume. I think I know where one is!"

"Okay, Mom," Ian said. He smiled a small smile, then a bigger one when he thought about Mrs. Land and the other teachers watching Doug more closely. Ian knew the teachers would watch Doug more than the other kids, but Doug didn't know it! That was like a secret! Then he thought about his party and began to grin from ear to ear. He wondered what kind of costumes everyone would wear and how much candy they would get from trick-or-treating. And the best part of all: Doug would not be there!

Ian kept expecting Mom to drive to the mall or some other store, but she didn't. He was really surprised when she pulled into Grandy's driveway. Maybe Grandy was going to go with them. While Ian was excited to see Grandy and Pappy, they didn't have any time to waste. It was Wednesday, and time was running out. He needed a costume soon. He and Justin unbuckled and bolted out of the car. Ian beat Justin to the front door and rang the doorbell.

Justin began to cry. "I wanted to ring the doorbell, Ian!"

he screamed. Mom slipped up behind Justin and whispered something in his ear that made him smile. Then he hid behind the huge pot of mums on the front porch. Pappy opened the door and saw Ian and Mom.

"Hey!" he said, giving Ian a big hug. He kissed Mom on the cheek and then looked around. "Where's Justin?" he asked.

"I don't know," Mom answered. "I guess he'll be here later. Let's go in, Ian." Ian raced in to find Grandy. Pappy glanced over to the flowerpots and saw the top of Justin's head. "I sure hope Justin gets here soon," he said. "Grandy just made a batch of cookies!" Pappy closed the front door.

As soon as Justin heard the door close, and "cookies," he sprang up and bounced to the door. He pushed the doorbell five times then jumped back behind the flowerpot. He hoped Pappy would answer the door quickly because he didn't want to miss out on eating cookies.

Pappy did open the door quickly. He looked around and said, "Who's here? Who rang my doorbell so many times?"

"*Boo!*" Justin yelled as he jumped up from behind the flowerpot.

Pappy pretended to jump back in fright. "Why, Justin, you scared me! Did you see who rang my doorbell and then ran away?"

Justin laughed and shook his head no. He ran and jumped into Pappy's arms and kissed him on the cheek. Pappy carried Justin inside and plopped him down in a chair at the kitchen table. Ian was already there, eating a warm chocolate chip cookie and drinking some milk. Grandy was standing behind him.

"Hey, I want a cookie!" Justin exclaimed.

"I knew you would," Grandy replied. Her hands were

behind her back and when she brought them in front of her, she had a plate with two warm chocolate chip cookies on it in one hand and a glass of milk in the other hand. She set them on the table in front of Justin. "Ta da!" she said. Justin grabbed a cookie and began devouring it. Grandy kissed him on the forehead.

Ian drained the last of his milk, then leaned back in his chair and rubbed his belly. "Ahhh, that was good, Grandy," he said.

"I've got something else for you, Ian," Grandy said. "Let me go get it." She walked back to the bedroom. Pappy sat down between his grandsons.

"What's that Justin?" he said, pointing to the window. Justin whipped his head around to look and when he did, Pappy swiped his remaining cookie. He put his finger up to his mouth and whispered, "Shhh!" to Ian. Ian grinned.

Justin couldn't see what Pappy had seen. He turned around to get his last cookie, but it was gone! "Hey!" he shouted. "Where's my other cookie?"

"The person who rang the doorbell five times and ran away came and got it," Pappy answered. He pointed to the back door and said, "He went that way."

"*I* was the one who rang the doorbell!" Justin said. Then he got a funny look on his face as he realized he had just con-fessed to the crime. "Oops!" Justin mumbled. But then he saw the cookie in Pappy's hand and squealed. Pappy handed him the cookie. Mom handed Pappy two cookies and a glass of milk. She saw Grandy walking through the den to the living room, so she stepped behind Ian and covered his eyes with her hands.

"What are you doing?" Ian asked.

"Grandy has something for you," Mom whispered to Ian. "Hold out your hands."

Ian obeyed his mother. Grandy placed the costume in his hands. He felt the soft fur. "Is it a kitten?" he asked.

"Sort of," Grandy said.

Mom removed her hands and Ian looked to see what he was holding. It was his leopard costume! "Wow!" he exclaimed. "Is this for me?"

"Actually it's for me, but I'll let you borrow it," Pappy answered smartly. Grandy looked at him and put her hands on her hips. Justin giggled.

"Yes, it's for *you*," Grandy said. "Go try it on!" Ian dashed to the bathroom with his costume. After a few minutes he came back to the kitchen with a huge grin on his face. The costume fit perfectly. He felt like a real leopard!

Pappy jumped back. "My goodness!" he gasped. "I've got to call the zoo and tell them one of their leopards has escaped." He hurried to the telephone and began punching numbers.

"Pappy, it's *me!*" Ian giggled. "I'm not a *real* leopard. I just look like one!"

Pappy put the telephone down and wiped his forehead. "Whew!" he said. "That really scared me. I better have another cookie to calm my nerves!" He grabbed another cookie and then grabbed two more. He gave one to Justin, who crammed it into his mouth before Mom could say no. Pappy held the other one up so Ian could see it. "Can leopards eat cookies?" he asked.

"I don't know," Ian said. "But boys can!" He grabbed the cookie from Pappy and grinned at him. He too stuffed the cookie in his mouth so Mom couldn't say no—and also so he wouldn't get chocolate chips on his new costume.

"Okay, boys, it's time to go," Mom said. "Ian, go put your clothes back on."

"I want to wear my leopard costume," Ian begged.

"No, it will get messed up before Halloween," Mom said. "After Halloween, you can wear it as much as you want."

"Even to school?" Ian asked hopefully.

"Well, no, not to school," Mom said. Ian frowned, and then Mom added, "Leopards aren't allowed in school."

Ian grinned. "I bet old Doug would leave me alone if I was a leopard!" He relished the thought of seeing Doug shrinking back in pure, wide-eyed fear.

"I'm sure everyone would leave you alone if you were a leopard," Mom said. "Leopards are mean, wild animals."

"Kory's not!" Ian said defensively.

"Well, he's the exception," Mom said. "Now go change your clothes before *I* act like a mean, wild animal!" Ian bounded off, snarling, and growling, and dashing out at imaginary prey.

"The costume seems to be a hit," Grandy said.

"Yes," Mom answered. "I just hope Ian doesn't get it dirty before his party."

"It will wash," Grandy said. "I didn't buy material that has to be dry-cleaned!"

"Thanks," Mom said. "And thanks for making it for him." She hugged Grandy and then Pappy.

Ian came out clutching his leopard costume. He stopped and gave Grandy a big hug. "Thanks for my perfect costume!" he said. "This will be my best Halloween and birthday ever. I *love* my costume! And I love you, Grandy!"

Grandy kissed Ian on the cheek. "I love you too," Grandy replied.

"What about me?" Pappy said. Ian wriggled away from

Grandy and turned around to hug Pappy. Justin came up behind Pappy and hugged him.

"Pappy Sandwich!" he giggled. Both boys squeezed Pappy as hard as they could.

"Ooof!" Pappy uttered. He reached out with each hand and managed to find the ribs of both boys. Then his fingers went to work tickling them! The boys fell to the floor laughing. They rolled over, bounced up, and dashed to the front door and out to the car. Mom gave Pappy a hug and kiss. Grandy and Pappy walked Mom to the front door and out to her car. The boys were already buckled in their car seats. Ian had put his leopard costume in the front seat so he, and Justin, wouldn't mess it up.

Grandy waved to the boys. "I love you," she said.

"We love you too!" the boys waved back.

Pappy walked over to the car and opened Ian's door. He slipped him one more cookie and winked. "I love you, Ian," he said.

"I love you too, Pappy!" Ian said, smiling. Pappy walked over to Justin's side of the car, opened the door, and stuffed a cookie into Justin's hand.

"Thanks, Pappy!" Justin said, smiling. "I love you!"

"I love you too, Justin," Pappy said. "You boys don't tell your mom about the cookies," he whispered.

"We won't," they whispered back. Pappy shut Justin's door as Justin popped the cookie into his mouth and waved good-bye. Mom got in the car, started it and backed out of the driveway. Everyone waved to each other one more time.

On the way home, Mom had to stop at the store to buy the ingredients for cookies. Ian wanted to make cats, bats, and pumpkins. Mom found cookie cutters in those shapes, and also black and orange icing, as well as sprinkles to liven up the cookies a bit. She also got eggs, flour, and sugar.

When they got home, Mom cooked supper. Dad got home and Ian ran to get his costume to show Dad.

"How about that!" Dad said. "We'll have a leopard and a pirate here on Halloween! Cool! I guess I had better be good, huh?" Ian and Justin nodded their heads in agreement and giggled.

"Supper's ready," Mom said. "We don't want to be late for church." Ian said a quick prayer and everyone ate their supper, although Ian and Justin were slightly full from all of the cookies.

Ian liked Wednesday nights. He enjoyed church and also the fact that he got to stay up later. Church was over at 8:00, his normal bedtime. But by the time they got home from church, and he took a bath and got ready for bed, it was usually about 9:00. Tonight was no different.

As Mom and Dad tucked their boys into bed, Mom reminded Ian that tomorrow night they would make cookies for him to take to school on Friday. Ian snuggled under the covers with this happy thought and Mom's kiss on his forehead and drifted off to sleep.

Birthday Cookies and Party #1

The next morning when Ian woke up, he remembered that he and Mom would make cookies after school. He couldn't wait! He hopped out of bed, got dressed, and brushed his teeth. He walked into the kitchen and saw Mom packing his lunch. She stopped and gave Ian a hug and kiss. "Good morning," she smiled.

"Good morning, Mom," Ian said. "Are you ready to make cookies after school?"

"Yes, it will be fun," Mom answered.

"We need at least sixteen cookies," Ian said. "Well, actually seventeen, including Mrs. Land."

"Why don't we make enough so everyone can have two cookies?" Mom said. "And of course, we'll make a few extra cookies for us!"

"That's a great idea!" Ian exclaimed. He heard Dad walking down the hall.

"Are you about ready for school?" Dad asked, hugging Ian.

"Yes, I'm just talking to Mom about making cookies tonight for my school party tomorrow," Ian said.

"What party?" Dad asked. He winked at Mom and then said, "It's too early for Christmas!"

"*Ahem!*" Ian cleared his throat loudly. "Cookies for my *birthday* party, Dad!"

"Oh, *that* party," Dad said. "Your birthday almost slipped my mind, what with leopards running loose around here, roaring, and making all sorts of noise! Let's go!"

Ian grabbed his lunch, kissed Mom good-bye, and headed for the car.

Justin had just woken up and was walking down the hall as Ian and Dad left. He asked Mom if she had already made the cookies. She told him they were doing it when Ian got home from school.

"Okay," Justin answered sleepily. He turned around, went back to his room, and crawled back into bed.

On the way to school, Ian told Dad about the cookies he and Mom were making this afternoon. "I'll make one especially for you, Dad," he added. "Mom said she'll make extras for our family."

"That's very nice of you, Ian, to think of your poor old Dad," Dad teased. Ian grinned.

They were almost to school when Ian looked at the car that pulled up in the lane next to them. He saw Doug, and Doug's baby sister, in the back seat. Doug saw Ian and stuck his tongue out at him. Doug's mom waved to Dad, and Dad waved back. He and Mom had met Doug's mother a few weeks ago at parents' night at school. Ian didn't remember seeing Doug's dad. Doug continued to stick his tongue out at Ian. Ian tried to ignore Doug. Just when he started to turn his head away, he saw Doug's mom reach back and snap her fingers at Doug. Doug quickly sucked his tongue back into his mouth.

Ian grinned before he could stop himself. Doug glared out the window at Ian, like it was Ian's fault. He continued to glare at Ian until a car in front of Dad stopped. Dad slammed on the brakes and Doug's mother passed them.

"Did you see Doug stick his tongue out at me?" Ian asked Dad. "This day is going to be great. I can tell already."

"His mom made him quit," Dad said. "Just think about that if he does it again." Dad turned the car into the school parking lot and drove Ian up to the drop-off door. Doug was already there. Ian kissed Dad and hopped out. He went inside and walked toward his classroom. He didn't see Doug hiding in the bathroom doorway, nor did he see Doug follow him to their classroom. When Ian got to his room, Mrs. Land was hanging up the pictures they had drawn yesterday. Reed, Ginger, and Jamie were there, but Ian didn't see Doug. Ian walked through the door, ready to tell his friends about the tongue-sticking-out incident. All of a sudden Ian felt a foot jab between his right foot and the floor. It lifted his right foot up a little and caused him to stumble into the doorframe.

Mrs. Land heard Ian bump into the doorframe and looked up. "Are you okay, Ian?" she asked. As she hurried over to help Ian, Doug shrunk back into the hallway. He waited a moment before walking through the door, pushing past Ian.

"Yes, I'm all right," Ian said, looking at his friends and rolling his eyes. *Naturally Mrs. Land didn't see Doug trip me,* Ian thought. *One more thing I can't prove.*

"Doug," Mrs. Land said. Doug had hurried over to hang up his coat and backpack. He stopped and looked at Mrs. Land. "Did you see Ian stumble?"

"No," Doug lied.

"Well, the next time someone near you trips or falls, you

need to help him or her, okay?" Mrs. Land gave Doug a very disapproving look. Ian could tell that now she had figured out that Doug was doing things to hurt him and his friends. *About time,* he thought. *I guess the little talk with Mom worked after all!*

"Okay," Doug muttered. Then he perked up a little and lied, "I was already past Ian. But I'll help him the *next* time he trips," Doug added, smiling at Mrs. Land. She walked past him and began hanging the rest of the pictures. Doug sneered at Ian. "Next time," he mouthed to Ian.

Ian gulped and looked at Reed. He sat down and began working on the math sheet Mrs. Land had put on his desk. Doug sat down, but Ian didn't look at him. He could feel Doug's beady, little eyes boring holes into his head. Luckily, other kids began arriving. *Now, Doug can focus on some fresh victims,* Ian thought.

Soon it was time for a spelling test. Mrs. Land called out each word and gave a sentence using each word. When she was finished, she took up the tests. While she graded them, she let everyone read. In a little while, she handed out the graded tests. Ian had spelled everything, including the bonus word, correctly. He glanced over and noticed there were a lot of red marks on Doug's spelling test. Doug stared at his spelling test. He looked up and saw Ian looking at his paper, so he popped his knuckles menacingly. Ian glanced away, but smiled to himself. *Doug may be mean,* Ian thought, *but I'm smarter.* He knew he would have to always stay at least one step ahead of Doug to beat him at his own game. And if the time ever came, he would have to muster up the courage to stand up to Doug.

The rest of the day crept by, even though Ian managed to

avoid any contact with Doug. At lunch, his friends all laughed when Ian told them about Doug getting in trouble in the car.

Finally, the bell rang, and parents arrived to get their kids. Ian burst out of the door as soon as he heard Mom. It was cookie-making time at last!

"Do you want to go to the mall or bookstore?" Mom asked Ian.

"No, I want to go home and make cookies!" Ian exclaimed. "I've thought about this all day!"

And make cookies they did! Mom measured the ingredients, and Ian added them to the bowl. He stirred the batter until it got really stiff, then Mom finished stirring it and rolled out the dough. Ian and Justin cut out the shapes and put them on the baking sheets. Mom popped the cookies into the oven, and Ian set the timer for twelve minutes. While the cookies baked, Mom rolled out more dough, and Ian and Justin cut out more cats, bats, and pumpkins. When the timer buzzed, Mom got the cookies out and put them on a cooling rack. She put the freshly cut cookies on the baking sheets and popped them in the oven. Ian set the timer for twelve minutes again. They did this again until Mom put the last batch of cookies in the oven.

"When this batch comes out and cools, we'll decorate them," Mom said. "You boys have about twenty minutes to wait."

"I'm watching TV," Justin announced and trotted to the den. Mom began running some dish water to clean up their cooking utensils.

"I'll help you," Ian said.

"Thank you, Ian," Mom said. It didn't take long, so Ian watched TV with Justin. They didn't hear the timer buzz or

Mom take the last batch of cookies out of the oven. She put all of the cats on one plate, the bats on one plate, and the pumpkins on one plate. She got out the orange and black icing and the sprinkles. Then she called the boys in to decorate the cookies. They dashed into the kitchen so fast that Mom didn't even have time to think about calling them a second time.

"Now, why don't you respond this quickly when I tell you to do something else, like put your underwear in the hamper?" she asked.

"Because this is *fun!*" Ian informed her.

Ian spread the icing on the bats and cats, while Mom iced the pumpkins. Justin got to put faces on the cookies with mini chocolate chips. He had wanted to put sprinkles on them, but Ian informed him that Halloween bats, cats, and pumpkins didn't need sprinkles. So Mom came up with the idea of using the mini chocolate chips. She whispered to Justin that he could put sprinkles on the cookies they were keeping. Justin snickered.

After all of the cookies for school had been decorated and wrapped up, Justin and Ian got to decorate the cookies left for the family. Justin handed Mom a bat with an exceptional amount of sprinkles on it. Mom bit off part of the wing.

"Mmmm!" she said. "These cookies are delicious! I *love* the sprinkles!"

"Fme, foo!" Justin said as he shoved half of a cat into his mouth.

Ian decided the cookies with sprinkles on them did look sort of cool. They tasted even better than they looked.

"You'll have to be careful with your cookies for school," Mom cautioned Ian.

"Maybe you should carry them in for me," Ian added. "I'd hate to drop them or fall on them."

"Okay," Mom said. "I just hope *I* don't drop them or fall on them!"

So the next morning, Mom carried the cookies for Ian. She did not fall or drop them. Justin carried the package of paper plates and Ian carried juice boxes. He told Mom that they had to have juice boxes. It was a party after all!

Mrs. Land let Ian keep the cookies on one corner of his desk. "We'll eat them after recess," she said. All morning, Ian would glance at the cookies. He couldn't wait until the afternoon! Everyone else made it a point to walk by Ian's desk on the way to or from (or both) Mrs. Land's desk to look at the cookies. Ian did notice that even Doug kept looking at the cookies with his beady, little eyes.

After what seemed to be an eternity, it was finally lunchtime. Everyone at the table chattered about the cookies and how they couldn't wait until recess was over so they could eat them. Doug didn't bother anyone at lunch or recess. He seemed to be in his own little world. *Good,* thought Ian. *Maybe even Doug is excited about eating the cookies, especially if he can swipe one from somebody. Hopefully this will make Doug act nice if he feels he's included in the party.* Ian hummed as he thought about how good life would be if Doug was nice. In fact, Doug was so quiet, everyone forgot about him. No one even noticed when he asked Miss Denton if he could go inside to use the restroom.

Once he was inside, Doug looked left and right, in front of him and behind him. He wanted to make sure no one saw him. No one was in the hallway, and all of the classroom doors were shut. He heard Mrs. Land and other teachers laughing.

They were in Mrs. Johnson's room, the second grade teacher, eating their lunch. Doug tiptoed past her room to his classroom. He quietly opened the door, like a burglar, and closed it just as quietly. He walked over to Ian's desk and looked back over his shoulder, verifying that no one was watching him.

Doug lifted the wrapper off of the plate of bats. He snapped off a bat wing. *Snap, snap, snap* went more bat wings. Soon the plate was full of wingless bats and batless wings. He covered the plate of broken bats and quickly unwrapped the plate of cat cookies. *Snap, snap, snap* went their tails. *Snap, snap, snap* went their legs. Now there was a plate of legless, tailless cats with a pile of legs and tails beside them. He wrapped up the plate of pitiful cat cookies and proceeded to the pumpkin cookies. *Snap, snap, snap* went the pumpkins. They looked like someone had thrown them off a building onto the sidewalk. Doug wrapped up the plate of smashed pumpkin cookies, and satisfied with his destruction, he quietly opened the door and crept back down the hall. He could still hear the teachers enjoying their lunch. No one ever knew he was in the building. He strolled out onto the playground and sat under a tree, waiting patiently for recess to be over.

Ten minutes later, Mrs. Land came outside and blew her whistle for her class to line up. She only had to blow it once, because everyone was ready for the cookies. She led them to the door and told everyone to use the restroom and wash their hands really well, whether they used the restroom or not. Doug grinned a sly grin, but no one was paying attention to him.

In the bathroom, while he was washing his hands, Ian noticed that Doug was washing his hands very thoroughly. He thought Doug's fingers looked blackish-orange, but looked away quickly when Doug caught Ian looking at his hands. As

Ian dried his hands, he tried to get excited about the party. *Even Doug won't ruin this day,* he thought.

"Okay, class," Mrs. Land said as they lined up to go to their room, "I'll pass out the juice boxes while you go to Ian's desk and get your cookies." She opened the door and felt something sticky on the doorknob. It was a blackish-orange substance. Before she could think about it, everyone hurried past her to their seats, anxious for their cookies.

Ian rushed over to his desk and picked up the plate of cats. He unwrapped the plate and froze when he saw the cats broken to bits. Frantically, he unwrapped the plates with the bats and pumpkins. They were in pieces too.

"Oh no!" Ian cried.

"What is it, Ian?" Mrs. Land said as she walked over to his desk. "Are you all right?"

"I am," Ian shouted, "but my cookies aren't! Someone has broken all of them to pieces! *Look!*" He held up a wingless bat. Everyone, except Doug, gasped in shock.

"I'm so sorry," Mrs. Land said. "I don't know who would do such a mean thing."

Ian jerked his head up and looked at Doug. Doug looked at Ian and quietly began mocking him. Before he could stop himself, Ian blurted out, "Doug did it!" Everyone shrank back in their seats.

"Prove it!" Doug answered angrily. He jumped up, knocking his chair over in the process. It landed on the floor with a loud bang.

"That's enough, boys!" Mrs. Land snapped. She looked at Ian. "Do you have any proof that Doug did this?" Filled with anger and sadness at the same time, Ian slowly shook his head.

His school party was ruined, thanks to Doug! But then he remembered Doug's hands when they were in the bathroom.

His eyes grew wide as he said, "Doug did have blackish-orange hands when we came in from recess!" Ian informed Mrs. Land.

Shock covered Doug's face. Defending himself, he yelled, "It was dirt!"

Mrs. Land looked at Doug. "Doug," she said firmly, "did you break the cookies?"

Doug looked at Mrs. Land, and then Ian, and then Mrs. Land again. "No," he said coldly.

"Do you know who broke them?" she asked.

Doug shook his head back and forth. "No," he added for emphasis.

"Did anyone see who might have come in here and done this?" Mrs. Land asked the class. Everyone shook their heads. No one had seen anything. Mrs. Land looked at Doug. "Well, whoever did this left some icing on the door knob!" She watched Doug for any reaction, but there was none. What were they going to do, call the police and fingerprint him or do a DNA test? She sighed and said, "Well, let's still have the party. We'll just eat broken bats, cats, and pumpkins. They'll still taste good." Everyone nodded, but the mood of the party had clearly changed.

While Mrs. Land passed out juice boxes, the kids filed past Ian, receiving a plate of bits and pieces of bats, cats, and pumpkins. Each child said something encouraging to Ian or patted him on the shoulder.

Doug was the last one in line. Ian had hoped he'd run out of cookies so that Doug wouldn't get one, not even a broken one. When Doug held out his hand for his plate of cookies and smiled at Ian, it was all Ian could do to not hit him. But he kept his composure. He searched through the pile of cookies, picking up the biggest pieces. He piled them onto a plate and held it out toward Doug, but to Doug's surprise, Ian walked past him and took the plate to Mrs. Land's desk. He came back, selected some more cookie pieces, put them on a plate, and set them aside. They were his cookies. Finally he picked up a few cat tails and tossed them onto a plate. He thrust the plate at Doug and smiled at him. Doug grabbed the plate and stomped to his desk. Alan and Mollie hid their smirks by wiping their mouths with their napkins.

"These cookies are really good, Ian," Jamie piped up from across the room. Everyone, except Doug, nodded their heads in agreement.

"They're really good," Tristan said.

"They're the best cookies I've ever eaten," Reed announced. "But don't tell my mom!" The class laughed. Ian laughed too. It was nice to have friends in difficult times.

In order to make the day brighter for Ian, Mrs. Land announced that they could spend the afternoon playing games or coloring. Ian smiled. He looked at Mrs. Land, and she winked at him. *She knows,* Ian thought. *She* has *to know that Doug broke the cookies.* He smiled a wider smile at Mrs. Land. Maybe the day wasn't totally ruined after all. In spite of the cookie disaster, Ian had a fun day. Everyone went out of their way to play with him.

Doug stayed at his desk. This day had not turned out like he had expected, either. He was so mad that Ian had accused him of breaking the cookies, even though he *had* broken the cookies. To make matters worse, no one was mad at Ian.

The afternoon flew by, and soon Mrs. Land was telling

everyone to pick up their toys and get ready to go home. Parents began arriving and soon Mom was there to get Ian.

"How was the party?" she asked. Ian hugged her and buried his head under her arm.

Mrs. Land came over and said, "We got off to a bad start, but everything turned out just fine, didn't it, Ian?"

Ian looked up and nodded slowly. Then he looked at his mother and said, "Someone broke all of my cookies!"

Doug's mother walked up just then. Doug raced to the door, pushing past Ian. "Let's go!" he said to his mother and hurried out the door.

"Oh my!" Doug's mother said. "Who would do such a thing?"

That evil, bratty beast you call a son, Ian thought. Doug turned around and pulled his mother's arm until she followed him out the door.

Mrs. Land waited until Doug and his mom were down the hall. "Ian accused Doug of doing it," she told Mom. "Ian said he saw icing on Doug's hands, and I found it on the door. But we can't prove it, because no one actually saw Doug do it. The cookies were fine when we left for lunch. When we came in from recess, they were broken to bits."

"Did Doug sneak in and do it?" Mom asked.

"I didn't see him go in," Mrs. Land said. "I didn't have recess duty. But I'll check with the teachers who had recess duty to see if he asked one of them if he could go inside. Still, we had a good party, didn't we, Ian?"

Ian nodded. "And I'm having two birthday parties this weekend! My friends are coming over tomorrow night to trick-or-treat, and then my family is coming over Sunday after church!"

"My, my," Mrs. Land said. "Three birthday parties. What a fun weekend you'll have!"

"Yes, and a busy weekend too," Mom said. "I spent the day making our house 'haunted.' It's all ready for the parties. Let's go, Ian."

"Well, Happy Birthday, Ian," Mrs. Land said. She thought for a moment and then said, "I'll tell you what, Ian, as my present to you, on Monday we'll switch desks. Okay?"

"Great!" Ian exclaimed. "Thanks, Mrs. Land!" He gave her a hug and they left.

Ian complained about Doug the whole way home. Mom told Ian that Mrs. Land had said Doug had some anger issues.

"What are those?" Ian asked.

"It means that Doug has some problems, and he's angry about them," Mom answered. "Maybe there are problems at home, or maybe he's really shy and insecure. Maybe he's just lonely. Whatever his problems are, I think Doug needs your prayers."

"*Prayers?*" Ian asked incredulously. "Do you think I'm going to *pray* for someone who treats me like Doug does?"

"Doug is *exactly* the kind of person who needs your prayers," Mom said softly. "I hope you pray for him. It can make a difference in his life."

Ian thought about it the rest of the way home. But he forgot all about Doug the moment he stepped into the house. Mom certainly had been busy. Streams of black crepe paper hung from the ceiling fan in the den—the swirling vortex of death! Creepy, silky spider webs with plastic spiders hung from the corners of the kitchen cabinets, lights, and in the windows. The fireplace was filled with the silky spider web and a big, black, fuzzy spider was in the middle of the web. There were little blinking eye lights in the fireplace and under the furniture. Owl and bat decals were in the windows and a giant mummy poster was taped to the front door. Toy rats were in the corners of the kitchen and den. Bats hung from the ceiling in the bathroom. In the kitchen, Mom had placed the plastic cauldron on the counter.

Dad had been busy too. He had left work early to come home and carve the pumpkins. They were on the front porch with candles in them, ready to eerily light up the porch tomorrow night for the trick-or-treaters.

Ian couldn't wait. The party would be a blast. The best part was that Doug wouldn't be around to ruin it!

Birthday Party #2

The next morning, since it was Saturday, Ian and Justin got up at 7:00 a.m. Mom and Dad were sleeping, and the rule was no television before 8:00 a.m. Ian was so excited about his trick-or-treat party that he couldn't sleep any longer. The boys zipped into the living room and turned on the television to watch cartoons. Soon they were laughing as loudly as they could. They didn't see Dad stagger into the living room. Dad cleared his throat, and Ian and Justin both jumped. Ian quickly turned off the television.

"Why is it," Dad grumbled, "that we have to wake you up for school, Ian, but on the day you can sleep late, you wake up at the crack of dawn?" Dad rubbed his face, then bent down and scooped up both boys, causing them to giggle even more. He carried them back to Ian's room and plopped them down onto Ian's bed. "Please play back here until your mother and I wake up."

"But you're awake, Dad," Justin informed him.

"Yes, but I would like to go back to bed and sleep some more," he said. "If you boys are quiet for one more hour, I'll make bacon and scrambled eggs. Is that a deal?"

"Deal!" Ian said.

"Deal too!" Justin agreed.

Oh, Happy Birthday, Ian!" Dad winked at Ian, turned around, and trudged back to bed.

The boys began playing with some of their toys. In fact, they got so busy that they didn't realize they had been playing for nearly two hours. Justin's tummy began to rumble. Ian's did too. He also thought he smelled bacon cooking. He walked into the kitchen and saw Mom stirring up pancake batter. Bacon was frying in the pan. Dad was busy scrambling eggs. Ian closed his eyes and took a deep breath. "Mmmm. Birthday pancakes, bacon, and eggs!"

"Yes, it's going to be a busy day so you need to start it off with a good breakfast," Mom said. She stopped stirring the pancake batter and gave Ian a hug. "And it's good to start the day off with a hug too. Happy Birthday, Ian," she said and kissed him. He smiled at Mom and then ran to the den to watch television.

In a little while breakfast was ready. "Let's eat!" Dad announced.

Everyone enjoyed their pancakes and bacon. They even helped Mom clean up the kitchen. It had to be super clean for the party.

"When do we get my cake?" Ian asked.

"We'll get it a couple of hours before the party," Dad said. "Don't worry. The time will fly by."

But to Ian the time didn't fly by. It dragged by. He played with Rascal and Baloo. He rode his bike. He tidied up his room. He couldn't take it any longer. "Dad, let's go get my cake," he said. "I'm about to go crazy!"

"Okay," Dad said. "I wouldn't want you to go crazy on your birthday!" So Ian, Dad, and Justin left to get the cake. They also had to get the hot dogs for the party today and hamburgers for the party tomorrow. Dad took the boys to get a soda, too. It was Ian's birthday after all, and it was also a way to kill time.

When they got home, Dad began grilling the hot dogs. Mom was getting the plates and napkins out. Everything was just about ready, except Ian and Justin!

"You boys had better get your costumes on," Mom said. "The party starts in thirty minutes!"

Ian and Justin hurriedly changed into their costumes. Mom came back to paint whiskers on Ian's face and a mustache on Justin. By the time the boys transformed into a leopard and pirate, Ian's party guests began to arrive.

Reed was the first one there. He was dressed like a pirate too. He and Justin immediately began dueling with their plastic swords and seeing who could say, "Aaargghh," the most.

Jamie was next. She was dressed as a fluffy, white cat, even though she was allergic to them. She had wanted to wear her tennis outfit, but Jackson had informed her he was coming to the party as a tennis player.

Tristan and Alan arrived together, looking like a pair of dice. They had managed to find boxes they could fit into and painted them white with black dots. The boxes had holes for their arms, legs and heads.

The doorbell rang. When Ian opened it, he found himself staring at a beautiful, but very pink, fairy. It was Ginger. Her dress was made out of pink sequins, and pink, glittery wings were attached to the back of it. She carried a pink wand with pink ribbons on it, wore pink tights and shoes, and had pink glitter sprinkled on her face. She carried a pink, plastic pumpkin with pink sparkly stickers on it.

"It wasn't pink enough," Ginger said, looking exasperated. Ian looked at the pumpkin and then at Ginger. His eyes started to hurt. He rubbed his eyes and noticed Mollie walking up the sidewalk. She was dressed like a cowgirl (the cutest cowgirl Ian had ever seen) without a trace of pink on her. *Thank goodness,* Ian thought. *Ginger's wearing enough pink for the whole town!*

Jackson was the last one to arrive. And he did dress like a tennis player. He wore sweat pants, a tee shirt, a headband and wristbands. When Jackson saw Reed and Justin dueling, he promptly began to duel with them, using his tennis racket as a sword.

When everyone was inside, Ian showed them around the "haunted house." They all oohed and ahhed at what Mom and Dad had done. Reed and Justin still poked each other with their swords. Pirating was more fun than a haunted house. Besides, Justin was a little scared of some of the decorations and fighting Reed helped keep his mind off of the scary things.

"Dogs are done!" Dad announced. "I don't mean Baloo and Rascal. I'm talking about the hot dogs!" The kids giggled and found their places at the table. Dad said a prayer and then began putting hot dogs on plates. After everyone had their food, Dad told them to go over and have Mom get them a drink.

"Who wants some slimy goo to drink?" Mom asked. She had put lime sherbet, lemon-lime soda pop, and ginger ale in the big plastic witch caldron. She used the skeleton arm ladle to dip out the slimy goo and plopped it into cups for everyone. The kids loved it and came back for more until all of the slimy goo was gone.

Mom made another batch for them to drink with the cake. She lit the ten candles on the cake, and everyone sang "Happy

Birthday" to Ian. Reed and Justin added *matey* to each line, which caused everyone to laugh so much they could barely finish the song. They did, but Ian was still laughing when he tried to blow out the candles.

He blew out four when Reed said, "Aye, matey. 'Tis the plank for ye if ye don't blow out yer candles!" With a huge burst of laughter, Ian blew out the other candles.

"Well done, matey," Reed said as he clapped Ian on the back. "I'd hate to see ye walk the plank on yer birthday!"

"Arghh!" growled Justin in agreement.

"I'm glad no one took a drink of slimy goo," Mom said. "I'd hate to see it come out of your nose!"

"Ooohh!" gasped Ginger. "Could that really happen?"

"Aye," said Reed. "Would the pink lass like to see the pirate do it?"

"*No!*" everyone shouted in unison!

"Then it really would be slimy goo!" Alan said.

While everyone discussed the possibility of slimy goo actually coming out of one's nose, Dad cut pieces of cake and put them on plates and Mom dipped up more slimy goo. Justin gobbled up his cake, and when he thought no one was looking, he snuck over to the cake and began scraping off the icing and eating it.

"Caught ya!" Mom yelled, grabbing Justin around the ribs.

"Arghh!" Justin screamed. "I'll be taking this booty with me," he said, pointing to the cake. "So get yer hands off me treasure!" Mom grinned and Justin giggled.

"There's more treasure that awaits you," she said in her best-whispered pirate voice, "out there, amid all the houses. Chocolate, gum, lollipops, and candy bars lie in wait, waiting to be discovered and taken!"

"Aye, then let's be off!" Justin said. He grabbed his plastic pumpkin and headed for the door.

"Line up and get a flashlight," Dad said. "And remember, no one runs off from the group. We all stay together." As each child went out the front door, Dad handed him or her a flashlight. Then in unison, they ran from one house to the next, collecting a wide assortment of treats. They moved together, like a herd of wild horses, running from house to house. Mom and Dad waited in the street, making sure no one was left behind and also giving the signal for the herd of kids to cross the street. Pirate swords waved, pink streamers fluttered, and horizontal tails followed their owners as the herd of trick-or-treaters snaked back and forth across the street. Flashlight lights bounced eerily up and down or shone into unsuspecting faces. Occasionally, the flashlights would actually be used to check the supply of candy in the treat containers. And amid all of the laughter and talking, Reed and Justin would throw in an "Arghh, matey," and cause the group to erupt in more laughter.

Within an hour, the herd of kids had slowed their gait to a walk. There were still some bursts of laughter, but everyone was ready to go back to Ian's house and watch him open his presents.

Just as they reached the front door, Reed piped up with one more, "Arghh," and then added, "Me feet are killing me!" The kids raced into the living room and flopped onto the floor.

Ian began opening his gifts. He got a stuffed tiger (with which Justin immediately fell in love), books, an ant farm (Mom was thrilled with that gift), a board game, and gift cards. Alan gave Ian a tin can of candy, and when Ian opened it to see what kind of candy was in it, a large springy snake uncoiled and shot up into the air. Ginger screamed like a banshee, causing everyone to jump as much as they did when the snake erupted from the can. They began to laugh and Ian crammed the snake back into the can. He aimed it at Reed and popped the top off before Reed could run for cover. Reed did the same, but aimed the snake at Ginger, causing her to shriek in fright again. Justin enjoyed watching her scream, and then remembered he had a pumpkin full of candy and promptly dumped its contents onto the carpet. Everyone else did the same thing and soon the living room floor was covered in various types of candy and the occasional orange or apple, which were promptly tossed aside.

"Who gives out fruit for Halloween?" Tristan asked, clearly bewildered.

"Probably some dentist," Jamie added. "I'm not going to waste my time eating some stupid apple," and promptly popped a mini candy bar in her mouth. Then she grabbed the snake can, aimed it, and fired it at Jackson. "Take that!" she said. But Jackson was too quick. He raised his tennis racket and backhanded the fake snake. It landed back in Jamie's lap with a sad thud.

As everyone sorted, traded, and ate their candy, they took turns shooting the snake at each other. The time passed quickly and soon parents began arriving. Ian thanked each guest for coming to his party and his gift. After everyone had left, he sifted through his presents again, more slowly this time, and ate a few more pieces of candy. It was bedtime and Mom came in just as Ian popped one more mini candy bar into his mouth.

"No more candy!" Mom exclaimed as she walked into the living room. "You've had cake and punch and who knows how much candy. It's time for a quick bath and bed!" Ian swallowed the candy bar as quickly as he could before Mom had a chance to tell him to spit it out. "And be sure and brush your teeth very, very well!" she added.

Justin zipped into the living room. "Can I have a piece of cake?" he asked Mom.

Mom turned around to give him a definite, "No way," and saw Justin's face. His lips and chin were covered with orange and purple icing. He had even managed to get a little bit of icing on his nose and in his eyebrows, as if he had dived head-first into the cake.

"It looks like you've already had some," she said. Justin stuck his tongue out and licked the icing around his mouth. "Brush your teeth extremely well too," she told Justin and turned him in the direction of his bathroom.

As the boys brushed their teeth, they were sure to scrub extra hard. They didn't want to get cavities or in trouble with Mom. And while they were brushing their teeth, Ian ran his bath water. After a quick bath, he drained his water and ran some bath water for Justin. After Justin had his bath, he and Ian came back into the living room, ready for prayers. They sat down on the floor, next to Ian's presents.

Justin picked up the stuffed tiger and squeezed it. Ian had brought Kory with him. Justin knew the tiger was Ian's and looked at him. As he handed the tiger to Ian, his bottom lip trembled a little. He folded his little hands and put them in his lap. Ian whispered in Kory's ear, and then made Kory nod his head up and down. He handed the tiger to Justin. "You can have the tiger, Justin," Ian said. "I've got Kory."

"Do you really mean it, Ian?" Justin asked, a big grin breaking out on his face. Ian nodded. Justin grabbed the tiger and squeezed him. "Thank you, Ian. Thank you for Scrubby!"

"Who?" Ian asked.

"Scrubby," Justin said matter-of-factly. "That's his name."

"Okay," Ian said. *What kind of a name is that,* he thought. *It doesn't matter. I've got Kory.* He gave Kory a big hug.

Mom and Dad came into the living room for prayers. "Look what Ian gave me!" Justin exclaimed, holding up Scrubby. Then he clutched him to his chest.

"How sweet of you, Ian," Mom said. She leaned over and gave Ian a big kiss on the cheek.

"His name is Scrubby," Justin said.

"What?" Dad asked.

"Scrubby," Justin said. Why did everyone have a problem with his tiger's name?

"Oh," Mom said. "Scrubby's a nice name."

"Thanks," Justin said. "I'll say my prayer first." He thanked God for Jesus, his family, and Scrubby.

Ian was next. He thanked God for Jesus, his family, and his fun birthday party. Then he quickly asked God to help Doug.

Mom and Dad said their prayers, too. After the last "amen," they whisked both boys off to bed. Justin bounced in bed with Scrubby.

"My Scrubby," he said, holding him tightly to his chest as Mom and Dad kissed him good night.

They came into Ian's room and tucked him in. "Happy Birthday, Ian," they both said. Mom kissed Ian and whispered thanks to him for giving Scrubby to Justin. When they left, Ian thought about his birthday. He had thought Doug had ruined the whole weekend when he broke the cookies yesterday. *Maybe Doug really does have some sort of problem,* he thought. But the party yesterday had turned out all right, and he had had so much fun tonight at his party. He was thankful for his home and also with the warm feeling he had in his heart from giving Scrubby to Justin. Then he remembered tomorrow was his family birthday party. His birthday wasn't over yet! He fell asleep with thoughts full of love and happiness.

Birthday Party #3

The next morning the boys woke up early. Since it was Sunday, they wouldn't have as much time to play, because they would have to get ready for church. Mom and Dad couldn't sleep late today! The boys crept into the den, and Ian began to read Justin one of his new books. They tried to keep quiet, but one of the books was really funny, and they kept giggling and then laughed out loud. When Ian finished the book, he got out his new board game. He and Justin went back to his room to play it.

"It's called Kaboom, Justin," Ian said. "It looks like it is going to be fun. I'll read the directions and see how to play it. Let's get really good at it, so we can beat Mom and Dad!" Justin smiled and nodded. He had Scrubby with him, so Scrubby could learn how to play the game too.

Ian read the directions. It seemed fairly easy. Each player had to set up a fort made of plastic blocks, put soldiers in the fort, load small plastic balls into a catapult, shoot the balls at the opponent's fort, and knock down the blocks. If one block was knocked down, one soldier advanced. If two blocks were knocked down, two soldiers advanced. The first person to destroy the opponent's fort and overtake it won the game.

By the time the boys had mastered Kaboom, almost a half

of an hour had passed. When they realized how long they had been playing the game, they ran down the hall toward Mom and Dad's room. The sound of cereal being poured into bowls made them stop. Mom and Dad were up.

"Thanks for letting us sleep in a bit," Dad said. "Now how about some cereal?"

"Sure," Ian said. "Then Justin and I want to team up against you and Mom and play Kaboom!"

Dad looked at Mom. "Sounds like we may get beaten," he said. Mom nodded. She was sure a defeat was in her near future.

They ate breakfast, and Ian set up the game while Mom put the dishes in the dishwasher. "It's easy," he said.

"I bet," Mom answered. "Remember, we only have time for a quick game."

"This won't take long," Ian said smugly. Justin giggled and covered his mouth with his hands.

Ian was right. From the very beginning, Mom and Dad didn't stand a chance. In fact, they were beaten so quickly in the first game that they had time for a second game. After another trouncing, Mom declared that she needed to get ready for church and that everyone else should as well.

After church Mom had just enough time to make Ian's favorite cake, lemon raspberry. While the cake was baking, Mom got out the plates and napkins.

Dad began grilling the hamburger patties. The boys followed Dad outside and played with the dogs. When Baloo and Rascal smelled the meat, they stopped playing with the boys and ran over to Dad. He had their undivided attention and made sure a few bits of hamburger meat fell on the ground. The dogs made sure those errant pieces of hamburger meat were promptly devoured. One piece of meat was particularly hot, but Rascal grabbed it anyway. He spit it out quickly, then pawed and barked at it until it was cool enough to eat.

By the time the hamburgers were cooked and the cake was frosted, Mom's family and Dad's family had arrived. Everyone was hungry and wanted to eat as soon as possible, but Ian wanted to open his presents first. No one argued with him, since it was his birthday.

Ian got money, cds, DVDs, books, and gift cards to his favorite smoothie place and bookstore.

"What did you get from your friends?" Valerie asked Ian. Ian rattled off everything he had gotten and laughed when Valerie squirmed as he told her about the snake.

"Do you want me to show you?" he asked.

No thanks!" Valerie answered. "You know how much I hate snakes. Real or fake!"

Justin showed everyone Scrubby and told them that Ian had given Scrubby to him. He gave Scrubby a big hug and kiss.

"That was sweet," Grammy said.

Ian nodded and then began counting his money. "I have sixty-five dollars!" he exclaimed. "I better put it in my piggy bank before it gets lost or caught up with the wrapping paper and thrown away." Ian grabbed his cash and headed to his room.

"Say, Ian," Pappy said, "could I borrow some money?"

Ian giggled. "How much do you need?"

"Oh, about sixty-five dollars!" Pappy replied.

Ian giggled. "You better ask Mom or Dad for that kind of money!" He zipped down the hall to put his money away before anyone else could ask him for a handout.

Pappy laughed and fished through the plastic pumpkin for

some Halloween candy. He found what he was looking for and popped it into his mouth. "When are we going to eat?" he asked.

"How about now?" Mom said. Everyone filed into the kitchen and held hands while Dad said the prayer. While everyone was eating, Ian told them about the events of his birthday, from Doug breaking all of the cookies to his trick-or-treat party.

"Doug must have a problem," Jennifer said.

Ian nodded in agreement. "He does, but Mom told me I should pray for him."

"That's probably a good idea," Jennifer said, "but he may need to be confronted too. Sometimes that's what it takes to make a bully be nice or leave you alone." She popped a chip into her mouth and crunched it at Ian.

Soon everyone began telling stories about bullies they had encountered and how the problems had been resolved. Ian felt better. He didn't realize that he was not the only one who had been tortured by a bully.

"Who wants some birthday cake?" Mom asked as she brought the cake into the dining room. Dad lit the candles and everyone sang "Happy Birthday" to Ian.

"Don't spit all over the cake," Travis said. "At least, not on the piece I'm going to eat!"

"I won't!" Ian giggled. He took a deep breath and blew out all ten candles. Mom had stuck them close together. When Mom began cutting pieces of cake, Ian and Justin grabbed two pieces of cake and gobbled them up. Ian ran back to his room to get Kaboom. When the game was set up, the boys called Pappy and Popu over to play the game.

"They aren't going to know what hit them, Justin," Ian said.

And they didn't. Ian and Justin thoroughly trounced their grandfathers, and then Rachel and Ashley. Travis hated to lose, so he didn't even volunteer to play Kaboom.

"Chicken," Andrea said. Ian and Justin giggled.

"Would anyone else like to play Kaboom with us?" Ian asked, giving Justin a high five. There were no takers. In fact, everyone was beginning to look sleepy. So they started the good-bye hugs and kisses and began leaving.

"See you later, alligator," Ashley said.

"Happy Birthday, Ian," Rachel said. She swatted at Ian's rump, but he twisted sideways and all she swatted was air. Ashley giggled.

"Nice try," Ian said.

"That's right," Popu said as he was leaving. "We forgot to give you your birthday spanking!" He reached for Ian, but Ian leaped away. Right into Pappy's arms!

"Now I've got you!" Pappy growled. "How about some payback for beating me so badly in Kaboom?" Ian tried to squirm away, but Pappy's arms were wrapped around him like a boa constrictor. Ian had a brief thought about how Exx's lunch victims must feel.

"One!" Pappy said and Ian closed his eyes, waiting for the spanking to commence. Pappy hugged Ian and Popu kissed him.

"Two!" Popu said as Pappy hugged Ian. Popu planted another kiss on Ian's cheek.

Ian now realized he wasn't going to be spanked. He relaxed and enjoyed the birthday love. Grandy and Grammy walked up, ready to give Ian kisses, too as Pappy continued to count.

Justin had been watching the whole "spanking" scene. He dashed up to Ian and shouted, "And one to grow on!" He swatted Ian on the rear and made a hasty retreat, giggling as he ran out the front door.

"Why, you little ..." Ian snarled, rubbing his rear end and looking around for Justin. But Justin was gone, almost to the neighbor's yard. "I'll get you on *your* birthday, Justin!" Ian bellowed.

"After his hugs and kisses?" Grandy asked.

"*You* can give him the hugs and kisses!" Ian exclaimed. He rubbed his hands together and then said in his most menacing voice, "But I will give him his spanking!"

Pappy hugged Ian one more time, "to grow on," then he and Grandy walked out to their car. Ian followed them out and watched everyone get into their cars and drive away, waving as they left.

What a great day this has been, Ian thought as he smiled and waved. Then he, Mom and Dad went inside. Justin was hiding behind the bushes so Ian wouldn't get him. He waited a few minutes then snuck quietly into the house and ran back to his bathroom to take a quick bath.

As Justin reached around to turn on the water, Ian, who was hiding behind the shower curtain, grabbed Justin's wrist. "*Ah ha!*" Ian shouted.

Justin screamed so loudly Ian's ears hurt. He jumped and tried to get away, but Ian had a strong grip on Justin's wrist. Justin had such a terrified look on his face that Ian began to laugh. He relaxed his grip, and Justin broke free, running and screaming down the hall looking for Mom. Ian kept laughing. He knew he had gotten Justin back better than if he had swatted him on his rump. And he hadn't had to wait until Justin's birthday, either!

"*What is going on?*" Dad bellowed as he stormed down the

hall. By now, Ian was sitting in the bathtub, still laughing. He tried to tell Dad what had happened, but was too tickled. He kept laughing, and soon Dad was laughing, although he wasn't sure why he was laughing.

Mom and Justin walked in. Justin was clinging to Mom's leg, hiding behind her, hoping Ian wouldn't see him. She stared at Ian and Dad with her mouth wide open. "Justin said you scared him, Ian," Mom said, attempting to bring Ian and Dad back to their senses.

Dad looked at Ian, and said, "That must have been some scare!" Then he resumed his laughter.

Ian finally caught his breath and said, "I only scared him because he smacked me on my rump!"

"Is that true, Justin?" Mom asked. Justin looked at his feet. He had neglected to provide Mom with that tidbit of information. Mom continued to look at Justin. Slowly he looked up at her and their eyes met. Justin nodded his head sheepishly. His bottom lip began to quiver, and his eyes filled with tears. He was in for it now!

"It was just a birthday spanking," he cried, hoping that would help his case.

"But it *hurt!*" Ian exclaimed. He had stopped laughing now.

"Okay," Dad said, "from now on, only Mom or I will administer any spankings. Is that clear?" Both boys nodded.

"But he *did* hit me!" Ian added.

"Yes, then you proceeded to scare the living daylights out of him," Mom replied. "I think you exacted your revenge." Ian grinned a little. He certainly *had* scared Justin.

"Now you two take quick baths, so you can get to bed," Mom said. She clapped her hands at them. Ian began running his bath water. No one was hiding behind the shower curtain to grab his hand! He chuckled to himself.

After their baths and prayers, Justin ran to his room and hopped in bed with Scrubby. Mom and Dad tucked Ian in.

"Happy Birthday, Ian," Mom said. She leaned down and kissed Ian ten times. She tucked the covers around Ian and Kory.

"Yep, Happy Birthday, ten-year-old," Dad said. He kissed Ian ten times too.

"Thanks for the parties," Ian said. "I had a great birthday! Maybe now that I'm ten I can start staying up later."

"Not anytime soon," Mom said. She turned off Ian's light. Then she and Dad went to Justin's room to tuck him in. Justin was already asleep, clutching Scrubby to his heart. Mom and Dad kissed him and went to watch television.

Ian was tired, but was still excited from all of his parties. He had a hard time falling asleep. He held Kory and thought about all of the fun he had had with his family and friends. He stared at the painted Kory, and then flopped onto his back. *Going to Kory's jungle would be a perfect end to a perfect birthday,* he thought as he closed his eyes and yawned. He didn't see the painted leopard leap off the wall.

Jerry

Thump!

Ian smiled. His eyes were closed, but he knew who was on his chest. He opened his eyes and stared into Kory's green eyes.

"Happy Birthday," Kory purred. Ian hugged the leopard's neck.

"Thanks," he said.

"You've had quite a birthday," Kory said. "*Three* parties! Are you too partied out to come to my jungle? We can wait if you're too tired," Kory teased.

"No way!" Ian said, pushing back the covers. He climbed onto Kory's back and dug his heels into Kory's ribs. "Ready!" he said in a loud whisper. With one huge lunge Kory went from Ian's bed through the tree on the wall and landed in his tree in the jungle.

As he looked out over the vast carpet of treetops, Ian let out a huge sigh. He was so happy to be back in Kory's jungle. He patted Kory and felt his chest vibrating from the purring.

"Let's go," Kory said and felt Ian hang on as he started down toward the ground. Ian felt something brush his back. *Probably leaves* he thought, but forgot all about it as Kory landed with a soft thud.

Suddenly Ian felt something sharp dig in to his back. He reached his hand back to grab the stick or thorn or whatever it was and felt something soft and furry. A cold, wet nose sniffed the back of his neck.

"*Aauugghh!*" Ian screamed. Kory jumped, and a flock of parrots squawked and flew out of a nearby tree. Ian leaped off Kory in a wild panic, grabbing and swatting at whatever was on his back. He craned his neck around to see if he had freed himself of whatever had sniffed him. Two round, brown eyes stared back at him. It was a squirrel.

"Hello!" the squirrel chirped. He wiggled his nose and smiled at Ian. "I'm Jerry." Jerry hopped onto Ian's right shoulder. Ian stopped flailing about like a mad man and stared at Jerry.

"Uh, hello, Jerry," Ian said. He was calmer now. "My name is Ian. Would you mind not digging your claws into my skin?"

"Oh, sorry," Jerry said. "My bad! I guess I thought you were a tree!" He laughed and snorted at the same time. An acorn flew out of his mouth, whooshing past Ian's cheek. It landed on the ground between Kory's front paws. "Oops," Jerry blushed. "I forgot I had that nut stuffed in my cheeks!" Then he remembered he was still clinging to Ian. Jerry released his grip and promptly fell to the ground. He twitched his bushy tail and darted to the nearest tree.

"Who did that?" he asked.

"Did what?" Kory asked.

"Knocked me off Ian," Jerry answered.

Kory closed his eyes as if he was in pain. "*You* did," he said, "when you released your grip." *Simpleton,* he thought. Jerry smiled at Kory and stared at him in total admiration, like Kory was the smartest animal in the world. Ian giggled. Clearly,

Jerry's wits were not as sharp as his claws. But he seemed really sweet.

Jerry dashed back up Ian's leg and perched on his shoulder. He looked down at Kory, and then spied the acorn by Kory's feet.

"Hey, an acorn!" he shouted. In a blurry flash, Jerry leaped from Ian's shoulder, scooped up the acorn and shoved it in his mouth. In another blurry flash of movement, Jerry ran back up Ian's leg and resumed his position on Ian's shoulder.

"Ow!" Ian cried, sucking in his breath. "That hurts, Jerry!"

Jerry twitched his tail and hid behind Ian's head. He peeked out and whispered, "Sorry," into Ian's ear.

"It's okay," Ian said, wiping his leg and checking to make sure he wasn't bleeding. He wasn't. "You have got to remember that I'm not a tree. I feel it when your claws dig into me!"

Immediately Jerry released his grip on Ian and fell to the ground once again. Ian scooped him up and cuddled him.

"I'll tell you what," he said. "I'll carry you in my arms, okay? No more pretending I'm a tree!"

"Okay!" Jerry said, nodding his head so fast Ian couldn't focus his eyes on Jerry. "Now, where are we going?"

"Beats me," Ian said. "Ask Kory."

In a flash, Jerry was standing in front of Kory, staring up at him with large, brown eyes. "May I go with you and Ian?" he squeaked. For added emphasis, he made his bottom lip quiver just a bit.

Kory sighed deeply. He was about as excited to have Jerry around as he was to have Mason around. *Thank goodness they both aren't here,* he thought. "We are just going to walk around the jungle, Jerry, to see what we can see," Kory said. "We aren't going to any place in particular. If it means that much to you to go with us, then come along. Besides, it's Ian's birthday!"

Jerry beamed up at Ian, smiling so wide that all of his teeth were exposed and his eyes squinted shut. "I didn't know it was your birthday," he said.

Kory rolled his eyes. As politely and patiently as possible (Jerry was extremely sensitive), he said, "How could you know it was Ian's birthday? You only met him five minutes ago?"

"Hee hee," giggled Jerry. "You're right, Kory." Again, Jerry looked at Kory with wide-eyed wonder, amazed at how Kory could be so intelligent. Yes, he was truly standing in the presence of genius. Suddenly, Jerry's tiny brain kicked into gear and he popped the acorn out of his cheek and handed it to Ian. "Happy Birthday, Ian!" he proudly proclaimed.

"Th-aa-anks," Ian stammered as he carefully took the slobber-covered acorn from Jerry. *What am I going to do with this,* Ian thought.

"If you want, I'll keep it for you until it's time for you to go home," Jerry offered.

"O—" Ian began. But before he could finish saying okay, Jerry swiped the acorn from Ian's hand and stuffed it back into his cheek. He smiled at Ian. Ian smiled back.

"Well, let's go see what we can see," Kory said, hating to break up the gift exchange. He and Ian started walking down the path.

Jerry scrambled up Ian's leg, forgetting that Ian wasn't a tree. He felt Ian wince under the pain. "Sorry," Jerry said, settling into the crook of Ian's arm. He was perfectly content here, staring up at the trees, waiting to see what they would encounter. Ian took his other hand and patted Jerry on the head. He began to tell Kory and Jerry about all of his birthday

parties, going trick-or-treating, his gifts, Scrubby, and then Doug breaking all of the cookies.

"Doug sounds like Binky," Kory noted. "I guess there's a Binky or Doug everywhere." Ian nodded in agreement.

All of a sudden, Jerry exploded out of Ian's arm and dashed up a tree screaming, "I got it! I got it!" Ian and Kory watched Jerry race out onto a branch and grab an acorn. He popped it into his mouth with the other acorn and jumped onto Ian's shoulder. He snuggled back into Ian's arm and smiled up at Ian.

"May we continue?" Kory asked, swishing his tail.

"Certainly," Jerry replied. "Don't mind me. I'm having a great time!"

Kory and Ian resumed their walk. Occasionally (Ian and Kory began to get used to it), Jerry would spring from Ian's arm, race up a tree, and grab a nut seen only by him. He would be back in Ian's arm before the boy and leopard took more than five steps.

After a while Kory stopped under a big tree. It wasn't nearly as big as Kory's tree, but it was still a big tree. Kory and Ian sat down.

"Hey, why'd we stop?" Jerry asked. His nose twitched.

"Just to rest a bit in the shade," Kory said. "It's starting to get hot."

"I'm not hot," Jerry stated. Then he ran up the big tree and zipped around. Surely a tree this big had lots of nuts.

"I don't think he can fit one more nut into his mouth," Ian giggled. "His cheeks are so full that his eyes are starting to bulge." Ian looked around and spied a small buffalo berry bush. He walked over to it and found a few ripe berries. He picked them and walked back over to Kory and sat down. He began eating them one by one to savor the sweet taste and also so he wouldn't look like a squirrel with cheeks bursting at the seams.

Kory stretched out on the ground. Ian finished his berries and then laid his head on Kory's back and relaxed. He could feel the vibrations of Kory's deep purring. Occasionally, leaves would float down, and they'd hear Jerry chuckle and bark as he found nuts. His sounds were becoming more muffled, though. Ian could only imagine how full Jerry's cheeks were becoming. He smiled and drifted off to sleep.

His eyes popped open a few minutes later as he felt the ground beneath him begin to tremble. More leaves drifted down, in larger numbers, and Ian knew Jerry wasn't finding that many nuts. Kory leaped up and grabbed Ian by the shirt. He slung Ian onto his back and bounded onto a branch in the big tree. Jerry zipped down to the branch where Ian and Kory were. His eyes were almost as big as his cheeks. Ian didn't recall when he had ever seen such full cheeks. He almost grinned, but was too concerned about what was making the ground shake. Jerry had no clue and hopped into Ian's arms.

Suddenly, Binky and his buddies crashed into view. They stopped beneath the tree, and Binky inhaled a giant gulp of air and then snorted it out. He smelled Ian. He looked up and saw them. His angry eyes narrowed to slits.

"What are you doing in my jungle?" he bawled.

"We're not doing anything," Kory snarled. "And it's just as much *my* jungle as it is yours!"

"*Liar!*" Binky bellowed. "I see the buffalo berry juice on the boy's mouth. He's been eating all of *my* berries!" Binky charged at the tree and rammed it with his thick skull. Kory dug into the branch with his claws. Ian fell but managed to hang on. His legs dangled below the branch. He frantically tried to swing himself back onto the branch. Jerry leaped onto Kory's back and looked at the water buffalo.

Binky saw Ian hanging from the branch. He smiled a wicked smile and then charged the tree again. Kory roared to try and distract Binky, but the crazy water buffalo kept charging. Just before he struck the tree, Jerry furiously spit an acorn at Binky, hitting him on the top of his head.

Startled, Binky stopped and looked up, fixing his eyes on Ian, who had managed to swing up onto the branch. He straddled it and hung on for dear life. Binky snorted and charged again, ramming the tree and hoping to knock Ian loose.

Kory bared his teeth and growled. He vaulted down in the middle of the other water buffaloes and slashed at them with his claws. They scattered like roaches, crashing and running in three different directions, bawling in fear. Now Kory focused on Binky. He didn't even notice Jerry, who had scurried down the tree trunk, stopping a few feet above Binky's head.

Jerry inhaled deeply through his nose and spit another acorn at Binky. It hit Binky between the eyes. He shut his eyes and bellowed. By now, Jerry had zipped up to the branch where Ian was still clinging and spit out another acorn. This one hit Binky in the rear end. Binky whirled around to see what had hit him. When he did, Jerry was ready. He aimed and fired!

Thonk! Thonk! Thonk!

Acorns and various types of nuts rained down on Binky. They hit him on the nose, on his shoulders, on his rear end, in his ribs, and one zinged into his ear. Welts formed where the squirrel's arsenal had struck him.

Ian lost count of the number of nuts Jerry fired on Binky.

How many more are in his mouth, Ian wondered. He looked at Kory, who was obviously wondering the same thing. Kory looked at Ian and Ian shrugged his shoulders.

They both looked at Jerry as they heard him take one more deep breath. Jerry narrowed his eyes and pointed to Binky. He had one acorn left, Ian's birthday present. Binky's eyes grew wide.

Patooie!

The last acorn torpedoed straight for Binky's head and landed squarely between Binky's eyes. Binky snorted in pure rage and then felt a swelling begin to rise between his eyes. He stared at Ian, somehow assuming he was responsible for this, and stomped his front foot. Then he crashed through the bushes beneath the branch where Ian was, and stampeded off through the jungle.

Ian swung down from the branch and dropped to the ground. He walked over to Kory and sat down. Jerry zipped over to where they were, hopped onto Ian's shoulder, and chuckled.

"I think I had better take you home, Ian," Kory said. "You're not going to be safe with an angry, acorn-riddled water buffalo around. And I doubt if the path is safe. Hop on my back, Ian. We'll have to travel through the trees to get you home."

Jerry sprang off Ian's shoulder and streaked to the next tree. "Race ya!" he laughed, taking off again.

"I bet he wins," Kory laughed. Ian nodded and giggled, hanging onto Kory. He crouched low on Kory's back, moving his hands forward on Kory's shoulders as Kory jumped from tree to tree. Ian felt like he was the one jumping. "Hey, that really helps," Kory called back to Ian.

When they reached the top branch of Kory's huge tree,

Jerry was already there. "Beat ya!" he exclaimed, chuckling to himself.

"What a surprise," Kory said.

Jerry cocked his head to the side. "It was?" he asked.

"Sure," Kory said. "I really thought I would win, since I was carrying a sixty pound boy and unable to move at the speed of light!" He smiled at Jerry. "I'm sure glad you were with us, Jerry. Maybe old Binky will think twice about messing with you or Ian!"

Jerry radiated pure joy from Kory's compliment. He flew over to him and hugged his neck. Then he remembered Ian and his birthday present. "Sorry about your present, Ian," he said, lowering his head. "I'll try to get you another acorn when you come back."

"That's okay, Jerry," Ian said. "You actually gave me *two* presents ... the acorn and hitting Binky in the head with it! Thanks! You made my birthday absolutely perfect!" He grabbed the squirrel and gave him a big hug. Jerry wrapped his little paws around Ian's neck and hugged him back. Kory purred.

"Let's get you home, Ian," Kory said.

"Okay. Good-bye, Jerry," Ian said. "I'll see you again. Soon I hope!"

"Bye, Ian! Happy Birthday!" Jerry grinned and then zipped off to find replacements for the nuts he had shot at Binky.

None of them noticed that Binky was lurking in the bushes beneath Kory's tree. "So he liked *both* presents from Jerry," Binky muttered. His body still hurt from being pelted with nuts and acorns. "Well, we'll just see if he likes the present *I* give him the next time I see him. Heh, heh, heh." Binky tromped off through the jungle, chuckling to himself and planning his surprise for Ian on his next visit to the jungle.

Ian hung on for the final jump through the tree into his bedroom. When Kory landed on Ian's bed, Ian slid off him and gave the leopard a hug. "Thanks for the fantastic birthday, Kory!" Ian said. "I had a great time!"

"Happy Birthday," Kory purred. "I'll come see you again soon." Ian closed his eyes, and when he opened them, all he saw was a painted leopard on the wall.

The Thumbtack Incident

Today is the day! Ian bounced out of bed before Mom woke him. He began getting dressed for school, choosing a brown sweater, jeans, and hiking boots. He hummed his way to the kitchen and rummaged around for breakfast. Ian was still humming as he fixed a bowl of cereal.

"Good morning, Ian," Mom said as she walked in the kitchen. She kissed him, and he continued to hum. "Why are you humming?" she asked.

Ian stopped humming, swallowed his bite of cereal, and answered, "Today is the day Mrs. Land changes our seating chart! I won't have to sit by Doug anymore!" He popped another bite of cereal into his mouth, smiled at Mom, and resumed his humming.

Dad came in while Mom packed Ian's lunch. "Good morning, Ian," he said, tousling Ian's hair.

"Hey, Dad!" Ian said. "I won't have to sit by Doug anymore! Mrs. Land changes our seats today!" Ian finished his cereal and put his bowl in the sink. He hurried to the bathroom to brush his teeth.

"So I guess things are getting better," Dad said to Mom.

"I hope so," Mom answered as she zipped Ian's lunch box. "Now if we can just keep Doug away from Ian on the playground, life will be a lot better!"

Dad kissed Mom good-bye. "Let's go, Ian!" he shouted. Ian came running down the hall. He grabbed his lunch from Mom and kissed her on the cheek.

"Bye, Ian," Mom said.

"Bye, Mom," Ian replied. "I'll see you after school." He was still humming as he walked out the door to the car. In fact, he hummed on the way to school. When Dad let him out, he kissed Dad good-bye and hummed as he hurried into the building and to his classroom. He sat down at his desk. In a few minutes, he would have a new desk and be sitting with a new group of kids! He couldn't wait!

Soon all of the kids, except Doug, were at school. Doug, as usual, was late. But when he arrived, Mrs. Land began reassigning seats.

"Let's see," she began, "Ian, you move over here. Jackson and Reed will sit with you." The boys moved to the new group and selected their desks. There was no fighting over desks. Ian breathed a sigh of relief.

Jamie was going to be seated in the group with Doug. She rolled her eyes as she moved to her new desk. Alan got moved to that group, too. He looked at Ian in disbelief. This was his second time to sit with Doug!

After everyone settled in at their new desks, Mrs. Land began their penmanship lesson. Today they were learning to write in cursive. When they finished their penmanship lesson, Mrs. Land gave everyone a bathroom break. As Ian stood up, he spied a thumbtack on the floor. He bent down and picked it up, and then raised his hand to tell Mrs. Land.

"Yes, Ian," she said.

"Mrs. Land, I found a thumbtack on the floor," Ian informed her. He held it up so Mrs. Land, and the rest of the class, could see it.

"Oh, just place it on my desk, Ian," Mrs. Land said. "Thank you for picking it up. I wouldn't want anyone to step on it and get hurt!"

Ian walked up to Mrs. Land's desk and placed the thumbtack on the corner of her desk. He was careful not to stick himself. He hated getting shots and sticking himself with a thumbtack would feel like getting a shot! He turned around and hurried to get in line to go to the bathroom. He was between Tristan and Ginger. He had no idea where Doug was, but was grateful he wasn't next to him. He looked around and saw Doug still sitting at his desk.

Mrs. Land walked to the front of the line and began to lead everyone to the bathroom. "Come along, Doug," she said.

Doug got up to get in line, but walked by Mrs. Land's desk on his way to the line. No one saw him whisk the thumbtack off her desk and place it in Ian's chair, pointy side up of course.

Reed was last in line, but as Doug got behind Reed, he didn't say or do anything to Reed. Doug was tempted to trip Reed, but didn't, because he didn't want to get into trouble and go to Mrs. Carter's office. He wanted to see what Ian would do when they got back from the bathroom. The kids filed out of the room and walked down the hall.

After everyone had used the bathroom and gotten a drink of water, they lined up to walk back to their room. Doug made sure he got in the middle of the line. Now no one could say he hurried to class and put the thumbtack in Ian's chair.

The kids were excited to begin their art projects. Mrs. Land had collected leaves, and they were going to get to decorate them with glitter and sequins.

"Oohh, Mrs. Land, do we have any pink glitter?" Ginger asked.

"I don't believe we do, Ginger. You know leaves aren't pink!" Mrs. Land replied.

"Well, my leaf is going to be pink!" Ginger announced. There was no way she was going to have a plain, ugly, brown leaf.

Mrs. Land looked around and found a small amount of pink glitter. She handed it to Ginger.

"Thank you so much, Mrs. Land," Ginger said, smiling happily.

"You're welcome, Ginger," Mrs. Land answered. "That's all of the pink glitter I have." She turned around and mumbled to herself, "But I guess I'll have to get some more for that kid."

"I'm going to give my leaf to my parents," Ian told Mollie as he walked to his desk. "Maybe my mom will frame it." He got the glue out of his desk and sat down, ready to decorate the leaf. "*Yowwww!*" Ian jumped up out of his chair as the thumbtack pierced through his jeans to his bottom. "Something bit me!" he screamed.

Mrs. Land hurried over to Ian. The whole class watched Ian jumping up and down, clutching his bottom. His fingers found the thumbtack and pulled it out. It looked like the one he had found earlier. He whipped his head around and looked at Mrs. Land's desk. The thumbtack was gone! "That's the thumbtack I found and put on your desk, Mrs. Land!" he exclaimed. All eyes were on Ian. No one noticed that Doug was grinning and chuckling to himself.

Mrs. Land's face grew very stern. She looked around the room and noticed Doug. "Class, does anyone know who put the thumbtack in Ian's chair?" No one knew, except Doug, and he wasn't about to admit it. All of the kids shook their heads no, even Doug.

"Who was the last one out of the room when we went to the bathroom?" Mrs. Land asked. Reed slowly raised his hand.

"Were you the last one out?" Mrs. Land asked.

Reed looked around nervously. He fixed his gaze on Ian, then swallowed, and said, "I was, until Doug got behind me." The smile quickly vanished from Doug's face, which turned a deep red.

"Doug," Mrs. Land said, "did you put the thumbtack in Ian's chair?" She put her hands on her hips and glared at Doug. Doug just stared at her. Ian was grateful to Reed, but felt sorry for him at the same time, knowing he'd be Doug's next target. Ian smiled weakly at Reed.

Mrs. Land continued, "I'm going to ask you one more time, Doug. Did you put the thumbtack in Ian's chair?"

"No," Doug said flatly without blinking.

Mrs. Land glanced around the room at everyone. "This is a very serious incident," she said. "We should not try to hurt our friends or classmates. I want each one of you to think how you would feel if this had happened to you. And if anyone knows who did this, I want you to tell me after school. It's not considered tattling or snitching. When someone gets hurt, whether it is an accident or on purpose, I need to know about it and who was involved. Are we clear on this?"

"Yes, Mrs. Land," everyone except Doug agreed and nodded their heads.

"Very well," Mrs. Land said. She turned to Ian and told him to go to the bathroom to see if he was bleeding. He nodded and hurried out of the room. Mrs. Land turned back to Doug. "Doug," she said, "I think you need to go to the office and tell Mrs. Carter what has happened."

Doug stood up, clenching his fists. He looked at Reed and gritted his teeth. Reed gulped.

"Go on, Doug," Mrs. Land said. She pushed the intercom button and told the secretary that Doug was on his way to the office. She heard the secretary sigh deeply.

Doug tromped out of the room, glaring at Reed one more time. Mrs. Land followed him to the door, and watched him walk to the office. She wanted to make sure he went to the office. Ian was coming out of the bathroom. He stayed on the other side of the hallway, avoiding Doug. When Doug saw Ian coming toward him, the smirk returned. Ian glanced at Doug, saw the smirk, and then glanced at the floor. He turned around to see where Doug was going and saw him walk into the office. Ian smiled a sly smile, but just as Doug was about to walk through the door, he looked back at Ian and saw Ian smiling. He clenched his fist at Ian.

"Come in, Doug!" Mrs. Carter said to Doug. He took his gaze off Ian and walked into her office.

Ian walked back to his room. Immediately everyone looked up and asked how he was. "I'm fine," he said, pleased that so many were concerned about him.

"Does it hurt?" Tristan asked.

"A little," Ian answered. "I'm not bleeding, though."

"That's good," Mollie said, smiling at Ian.

"We're all glad you're okay, Ian," Mrs. Land said. "You can start to work on your leaves now." Ian nodded and went to his desk, making sure there wasn't a thumbtack in his chair before he sat down. There wasn't. Of course not, because Doug wasn't there. He selected gold and red glitter for his leaf, dribbled glue on the leaf, and then shook the glitter onto the glue.

"Class, when you finish your leaves, you can bring them to me," Mrs. Land said. "I'll be at my desk grading papers."

Reed was the first one to finish. He walked to Mrs. Land's desk and gave her his leaf. "Very nice, Reed," she said.

"Thank you," Reed replied. When he got back to his desk, he apologized to Ian. "Sorry I didn't catch Doug."

"That's okay, Reed," Ian said. "It's not your fault that he's so mean. But be careful now. He'll probably try to get back at you for telling Mrs. Land he was last in line. Thanks for telling the truth and sticking up for me, Reed." Reed looked at Ian and gave him the thumbs-up sign. Ian grinned and then sprinkled some more glitter on his leaf.

Several more kids finished their leaves and gave them to Mrs. Land. Each child came by and said something nice to Ian. Ginger whispered something to Mrs. Land. Mrs. Land nodded. Ginger walked over to Ian's desk and gave him her pink, glittery leaf.

"Thanks, Ginger," Ian said. He smiled at her and then looked at the leaf. He had never seen a pink leaf before. Ginger had made the most of the small amount of pink glitter and had managed to cover nearly every inch of the leaf with pink glitter.

"I have a bandage with a pink pony on it if you need it," Ginger whispered to Ian.

"I'm okay," Ian said. "Thanks for the offer." It was bad

enough sitting on a thumbtack. Ian surely didn't want further humiliation by having a pink pony bandage on his rear end, even though he knew Ginger meant well. He smiled at her again, and she skipped back to her desk.

Doug came back and sat down. His face was red, and he didn't look at anyone. He grabbed some glue, squirted it on his leaf, and then threw some green glitter on it. He was finished with his art project. He grabbed the leaf and got up to take it to Mrs. Land. He did not go past Ian's desk after he gave Mrs. Land his leaf, which was still dripping glue.

He went back to his desk and sat down. He did not look at anyone or say anything to anyone. In fact, for the rest of the day, he left everyone alone, with the exception of glaring at Reed or Ian whenever he caught them looking at him.

Ian was more than ready to go home by the end of the day. When Mom arrived, he could barely wait to get to the car and tell her what had happened. As he was getting his backpack ready to go, Doug's mother arrived. Mrs. Land walked over to her and whispered something to her. Doug's mother walked over to Doug's desk and took a seat next to Doug. *Evidently they were going to have a talk with Mrs. Land,* Ian thought. *Good. She needs to hear how mean her son is to everyone.* Ian put on his coat and followed Mom out of the room.

Thanksgiving

Today was the day before Thanksgiving break and school was out at noon. For the past few days, Ian and his class stayed busy learning about turkeys, Pilgrims and Indians, and what Thanksgiving was really about. Doug stayed busy by continuing his personal tirades against his classmates. He had to be a little more discreet, since Mrs. Land always seemed to be watching him. But no one was safe. Doug found things to do to everyone.

Since today was a short day, Doug hadn't really had time to do anything to anyone. Most of the morning had been spent watching the fifth graders perform a Thanksgiving play. The rest of the day was set aside for a party!

Mrs. Land had made turkey-shaped cookies. She kept them behind her desk, hidden from sight. When the kids returned to their room after the play and sat down at their desks, Mrs. Land gave each child a cookie on a paper plate with Pilgrims on it. Ian looked at his cookie and noticed how plain it was. It had no icing or sprinkles. It was just a plain, naked sugar cookie. He wasn't the only one staring at his cookie. Mrs. Land expected this.

"Okay, class," she said. "I thought I'd give you a special

treat." She got a covered picnic basket from behind her desk. She walked over to a group, opened her basket and placed small tubes of icing and small cups of sprinkles in the middle of the desks. She did the same with the other groups. To Ginger's delight, Mrs. Land put a tube and container of pink icing and sprinkles on her desk. She knew Ginger would make a pink turkey. "Have fun decorating your cookies!" she said, smiling at everyone. "I'm going to pass out juice boxes while you decorate your cookies. Then, when you are finished eating, we will go around the room and each one of you will tell the class what you are thankful for."

"How cool is this?" Alan exclaimed.

Ian grabbed the tube of brown icing and covered his turkey. He used red and green icing for the tail feathers and shook colorful sprinkles on them. Satisfied with his decorating, he bit the turkey's feet off and grinned. The cookies were delicious.

While Ian and Reed were eating their cookies, Reed whispered to Ian, "Doug is probably thankful that he didn't go to the office today!"

Ian giggled, covering his mouth with his hands so cookie bits wouldn't fly out! He nodded in agreement. "And I'm thankful I don't have to sit by Doug!" Ian whispered back to Reed. They both giggled. Ian turned his head to look and see what Doug was doing, making sure that Doug wasn't standing behind him, ready to grind him into dust.

Doug wasn't standing behind Ian preparing to grind him into dust. He was sitting at his desk, staring at his cookie. He had only put a little bit of icing on it. There were no sprinkles on it. Doug wasn't bothering anyone. He just sat there and stared at his cookie, not like he was trying to figure out what it was or what it was made of, but more like he was looking at it but not seeing it. He seemed to be someplace else. Someplace that was lonely or sad.

"Okay," Mrs. Land said, oblivious to Doug's deep thoughts. "Let's begin telling each other what we are thankful for. I'll start. There are so many things to list it could take all day! But I'll just mention a few things: good health, America, and this class!" She smiled at everyone and then looked at Jamie. "Why don't you go next?" she asked.

Jamie stood up and told everyone that she was thankful for her family and ice cream. Alan was thankful for dogs, his parents, and toys. Other kids stated they were thankful for pizza, DVDs, hamburgers and French fries, swimming pools, horses, summer vacation, and bicycles. When it was Ginger's turn, she was thankful for her parents and all things pink.

Now it was Doug's turn. He hadn't made a sound. He just stared at his cookie.

"Doug," Mrs. Land said brightly, "tell us what you are thankful for, please."

Doug continued to stare at his cookie. Then he mumbled something. No one heard what he said.

"What was that, Doug?" Mrs. Land asked. "I'm afraid we didn't hear you."

Doug mumbled again, a little bit louder, but kept his eyes on his cookie. He snapped the turkey's head off and shoved it in his mouth.

"I'm sorry, Doug," Mrs. Land said. "We still didn't hear you. Please speak up."

Doug swallowed the bite of cookie. He looked at Mrs. Land. Obviously she wasn't going to let anyone else say what they were thankful for until he had informed the class of his list of thanksgivings. "Nothing!" he said. He took another bite of cookie and stared at the rest of the class.

Unsure of what to do, Mrs. Land smiled at Doug. "Well, Doug," she said, "perhaps you can't think of anything right now. But if you think of something later, please tell us." Doug took another bite of his cookie and nodded slowly as he chewed.

A few more kids said what they were thankful for, and then it was Ian's turn. "I'm thankful for God, my family, and America." He looked at Doug and then added, "And my friends." Doug looked at Ian, and then what was left of his cookie. He popped it into his mouth and stared at Ian while he chewed. Ian looked away and began talking to Reed.

In a little while, Mrs. Land told the class it was time to clean up the room and get ready to go home. She gathered up the icing and sprinkles and put them back into the picnic basket. Each child had to wipe off his or her desk. By the time the room was clean, it was noon. Parents were arriving. Doug's mother arrived, but he had not cleaned his desk.

"Grab a paper towel, Doug, and please wipe off your desk," Mrs. Land told him. "You don't want to have a sticky desk on Monday!"

Ian had just finished cleaning his desk. On his way to the trashcan, he swiped Doug's desk a few times with his wet paper towel. Doug's mom smiled at Ian. "Thank you!" she said. Ian was hoping Doug would be thankful that he had wiped off his desk and wouldn't be mean to him when school started back on Monday.

"Yes, thank you, Ian!" Mrs. Land said, smiling at Ian. She looked toward the door. "Here's your mother!"

Ian forgot all about thankless Doug. He was out of school for four and a half days! And he was thankful for that, too!

"Happy Thanksgiving!" he shouted as he left. He couldn't wait to get to the car and tell Mom about Doug.

"Hmmm," Mom said as she started the car engine. "Maybe there's something going on with Doug. It sounds like he needs your prayers more than ever, Ian. I mean, to say he has *nothing* to be thankful for makes me wonder what is going on at his house. He could have at least said he's thankful for food or his family."

"Or he could at least be thankful he's out of school until Monday," Ian noted. "I know *I'm* thankful for that! He sank back in the seat and closed his eyes. *No school for four and a half days! No Doug for four and a half days!* Ian kept his eyes closed until he heard Mom turn off the engine. He opened his eyes, grabbed his backpack, and opened the door.

"Hey, we aren't at home!" he exclaimed.

"No, we're not," Mom said. "How about some lunch?" They were at their favorite chicken nugget restaurant.

"Hooray!" Ian and Justin shouted. They bounded out of the car. Besides good chicken nuggets, the restaurant had a great playground.

Mom ordered while the boys played. When their food was ready, Mom called the boys over to eat. "First go wash your hands," she said.

Justin and Ian ran to the bathroom. While they were there, they decided it would be great fun to splash each other with water. They came out of the bathroom with water all over their faces and shirts. Justin's hands were still wet so he flicked water on Ian one last time and giggled. Then he began eating his nuggets.

"No more playing in the water, Justin," she said, scolding him a bit. "It is November and pretty chilly outside."

The boys gobbled up their chicken and raced back to the playground for a while. Eventually it was time to leave. Mom had to cook supper and make pies for Thanksgiving tomorrow. And it was Wednesday night. They had to go to church.

When they got home, Dad was just pulling up in the driveway. His office had closed early. He was glad, because his brothers from out of town and their families were coming in for Thanksgiving. They were going to have Thanksgiving at Grammy and Popu's.

Ian was so excited. This was going to be a fun Thanksgiving. School was out, Dad was home, and his cousins were here! But now he was going to watch television and play with Rascal and Baloo until supper.

When it was time for supper, Ian came in and washed his hands. He began telling Dad about Doug, the cookies, and the fifth grade play. He also told Dad how Justin had flicked water on him at lunch.

"Speaking of water, you two need baths before church," Mom announced.

"I'm first!" Ian yelled, running down the hallway to the bathroom. He took a quick bath and then watched television while Justin took a bath.

At church, Ian told his teacher about Doug. She decided the class needed to say a prayer for Doug. And after church, as a special treat, Dad stopped for ice cream!

When they got home, it was past Ian's bedtime, even though the next day wasn't a school day.

"I want to stay up late," Ian argued with Mom. Then he yawned.

"You need to go to sleep, so you'll be all rested and able to play with your cousins tomorrow," Mom said. She and Dad whisked the boys off to bed and tucked them in.

Just before Ian went to sleep, he looked at the painted leopard on his wall. "I wonder when I'll go back to Kory's jungle," he whispered to his stuffed Kory. Ian said a silent prayer. He asked God to let Doug find something to be thankful for.

The next morning Ian woke up and turned on the television. The Thanksgiving parade was on. In a few hours they would go to Grammy's house, and he could play with his cousins. He couldn't wait! The really cool thing was that all of his cousins were close to his age. Conrad and Wyatt were eleven and nine. Andrew, Coco, and Timothy were eight, six and three.

When everyone got to Grammy and Popu's house, it was wild. Kids were everywhere! Since it wasn't too cold outside, the kids were able to play in the backyard until it was time to eat.

When it was time to eat, Ian couldn't believe how much food there was. The table was covered with bowls and platters of food: turkey, dressing, green beans, corn, bread, potatoes, and some kind of broccoli casserole that Ian was not going to touch. For dessert, there was chocolate cake, a coconut cake, brownies, a pumpkin pie (which went untouched by *all* of the kids), and Mom's cherry pie, Ian's favorite. He had two pieces of cherry pie and then was ready to play some more with his cousins.

Ian was having so much fun with his cousins that he didn't want to leave. He was really excited to find out that all of his cousins were coming to his house to spend the night! It would be a giant sleepover!

When they got home, Dad got out two air mattresses and

inflated them. He put them in Justin's room for Andrew and Timothy to sleep on. Conrad was going to sleep on the top bunk in Ian's room, and Wyatt wanted to sleep on a sleeping bag on the floor in Ian's room. (He wanted to join the army and thought he had better practice sleeping on the ground.) Coco would have to sleep in the guest room with her parents, Russell (Dad's brother) and Cheryl. Conrad and Wyatt's parents, Gary (Dad's other brother) and Amy, were going to stay with Grammy and Popu.

The next day after a big breakfast of pancakes and bacon, everyone went to the zoo. The sleepover was repeated again that night. On Saturday, everyone came to Ian's house. The kids got to play most of the day. By late afternoon, Russell and Gary and their families had to leave to drive home. They wanted to miss the traffic on Sunday.

"We'll see you at Christmas," Russell said to Dad, giving him a big hug.

Sunday was a quiet day. Ian went to church, came home and ate lunch (turkey sandwiches), and then relaxed. Ian knew tomorrow he would have to go to school. He hoped Doug had had a good Thanksgiving. Except for telling his cousins and Sunday school teacher about Doug, this was the first time Ian had thought about Doug. He had had too much fun to ruin it by thinking or worrying about Doug.

Ian decided to go take a nice, long, hot bath. He thought about Doug some more and hoped he wouldn't be mean to him tomorrow. He almost fell asleep in the bathtub, so he got out and put on his pajamas. He brushed his teeth and walked out of the bathroom. Mom was on her way back with Justin. It was his turn for a bath.

Ian got into his bed and read a book. When Justin was

ready for bed, Mom came in to tuck her boys into bed. She kissed them both and turned out the lights. Ian didn't realize how tired he was until he got into bed. He had had a busy, but fun, weekend.

But now that it was dark and quiet, Ian began to worry about Doug again. He looked at the painted Kory on the wall.

"I miss you," he whispered softly. He said a quiet prayer and remembered to ask God to watch over Doug and help him with whatever problem he had. Ian closed his eyes and took a deep breath. He smiled as he felt a familiar thump on his chest. He was going to go to Kory's jungle tonight!

Justin Goes to Kory's Jungle

"Hello," purred Kory.

"Hello, Kory," Ian said as he ran his hands through Kory's thick, soft fur. "I was just wondering if I'd ever see you again."

"Well, you've been busy!" Kory exclaimed. "Every time I've checked on you, you've either had a bunch of kids in here or you've been fast asleep! I knew you were tired tonight too, but I just had to see you!"

"I'm glad," Ian said as he sat up in bed. "I've missed you!"

"Me too," Kory said. "And, uh, I have a favor to ask you."

"Just name it," Ian said.

"Well, do you see that tiger in the bushes on your wall?" Kory asked. He pointed a paw toward the tiger.

"Yes, I see it," Ian said, looking at the tiger. He turned and looked at Kory. "What's so special about it?"

"That's where the favor comes in," Kory answered. "The tiger is my friend, Scrubby. He has seen you with me in the jungle and wants a boy to do things with in the jungle too."

"Well, he can come with us like Mason did," Ian said. "I don't mind. Your problem is solved."

"Actually, it's not," Kory said. "Scrubby wants a boy of his *own*. Do you think Justin would want to come with us to the jungle?

"I don't know why he wouldn't," Ian replied. "I'll go get him!" He hopped out of bed and quietly hurried to Justin's room. Kory slunk back into the shadows, so Justin wouldn't see him. He looked at Scrubby and nodded. Scrubby nodded back and shivered with excitement.

Justin was almost asleep. He was gently tapping his hands on his chest. His eyes were barely open. He sighed heavily as Ian tapped him on the shoulder. "Are you asleep?" Ian whispered.

"Almost," Justin said sleepily. "Your talking has kept me awake. Who are you talking to? Is Mom in there?"

"No, she's not," Ian answered. He giggled a bit. "I've been talking to Kory and I'm getting ready to go to his jungle. He has a tiger friend, Scrubby, who wants you to come to the jungle with us. Would you like that?"

Justin's eyes popped open. "Sure I would!" he exclaimed.

"Shhh!" Ian clamped his hand over Justin's mouth. "Do you want Mom and Dad to come in here and ruin everything?"

"Sorry," Justin whispered. He grabbed his glasses off the bedside table and flipped the covers back, sending the stuffed Scrubby flying off the bed. Justin reached for the stuffed tiger.

"You don't need him," Ian answered. "In a minute, you are going to meet the *real* Scrubby!"

Justin zipped across the hall to Ian's room. "Well," he asked, looking around the room, "where is he?"

"Lie down on my bed and close your eyes," Ian said.

Before Justin could get to Ian's bed, an orange and black blur streaked from the wall to Justin, almost knocking him over. Scrubby was standing on his hind legs with his huge paws on Justin's shoulders. He licked Justin on the back of the neck. It tickled. Justin giggled, turned around, and gave Scrubby a huge hug.

"I'm Justin," he said, grinning at the huge tiger.

"It's nice to meet you, Justin. I'm Scrubby," Scrubby said. He gave Justin another big lick with his tongue.

"Well, if we're ready, then let's go!" Kory said. Ian hopped onto Kory's back and in a flash they disappeared through the wall.

"Hop on and hang on, Justin," Scrubby said. Justin did, scrunching his eyes closed as the tiger rushed toward the bushes painted on the wall. But instead of hearing himself smack against the wall, Justin heard leaves rustling and parrots squawking. He opened one eye slowly and then the other one. He was in a jungle!

Justin looked around for Ian and Kory, but didn't see them. He was about to ask Scrubby where they were when Scrubby looked up and said, "Here comes your brother."

As Justin looked up, he saw Kory sailing down from the top of the biggest tree he had ever seen. Ian was smiling and hanging on, clearly enjoying the ride. Kory landed almost silently next to Scrubby. Ian hopped off and told Justin, "I thought you'd be right behind us, but Kory reminded me that tigers don't climb trees!"

"But they're good at jumping through bushes," Justin added. He whispered to Scrubby, "It's just as well that tigers don't climb trees, because I'm afraid of heights!"

"Me too!" Scrubby nodded in agreement. "I prefer to swim!"

Justin gave Scrubby another big hug. Scrubby nuzzled Justin's leg so hard with his large head that Justin almost fell off the tiger.

"Where to first?" Kory asked.

"Justin has to try a buffalo berry!" Ian exclaimed.

"And there's some right by a nice pool," Scrubby said. "I'd love to take a dip in the water!"

"'Cause tigers like to swim," Justin added.

"We sure do," Scrubby replied. "What about you? Do you swim?"

"I love to," Justin said. "My mom had me take swimming lessons!"

"Let's go then," Ian said. "It's this way, isn't it Kory?" Ian turned right onto the trail.

"Yes, just follow the trail," Kory answered.

Justin started to climb off Scrubby, but a big orange paw pushed him back. "Just stay on and enjoy the view," Scrubby said. Justin smiled and nodded, settling in on Scrubby's huge back. He felt the tiger's powerful muscles rippling beneath his legs. He was actually riding a tiger! How cool was that? Justin kept grinning and looked around. He saw all kinds of birds and heard all sorts of sounds. He looked ahead and saw Ian and Kory, talking as they walked along. Ian had his hand on Kory's left shoulder. Justin was enjoying all of the sights as well as Scrubby's rhythmic walk. He reached down to pet Scrubby, but his hands never made it to their destination. Two long, strong, hairy arms grabbed Justin under his armpits and hoisted him off Scrubby.

"*Aauugghh!*" Justin screamed, reaching for Scrubby, and finding nothing but air.

"Hey!" Scrubby snarled, swiping at whatever was taking Justin.

Kory and Ian turned around. Kory looked up and saw what had Justin. He put a paw to his eyes and groaned, "Oh, no!"

"What, er, who is it?" Ian asked.

"It's Mason," Kory said. "And he's brought friends."

As if on cue, Mason popped his head out of the tree. He crossed his eyes and made a goofy sound at Justin, who was still screaming. When he saw the silly monkey, Justin stopped screaming. Mason uncrossed his eyes and scratched his head. "Wait a minute," he said. "You're not Ian."

Instantly another monkey popped out of the leaves and looked at Justin. In fact, he didn't just look at Justin; he brought his hairy face right up to Justin's and pressed his flat nose against Justin's nose. The monkey looked directly into Justin's eyes as his warm banana-smelling breath fogged Justin's glasses. Justin began to giggle, and all traces of fear vanished.

"You're not Ian?" the monkey asked.

Justin shook his head no. "I'm Justin," giggling as he said it. "What's your name?"

"Hector," the monkey replied. Hector looked at Mason. "This is *Justin*. He's *not Ian*," he told Mason, as if Mason hadn't heard Justin a moment ago. At this momentous revelation, three more monkey heads popped out of the tree leaves. One twitched his nose from side to side. The other two looked from Mason to Hector, like they were watching a tennis tournament.

"But," Mason began to stammer, "Ian *always* rides Kory or walks next to him." He scratched his head, clearly perplexed.

Kory rubbed his eyes again and sighed deeply. "Oh brother," he mumbled. "*Ahem!*" Kory said loudly. Mason whipped his head around to see who had made the sound. Kory and Ian waved to him. Mason smiled and waved back. The other monkeys waved, too.

"Hi, Ian!" Mason yelled. He slowly lowered his hand as a very confused look appeared on his face.

"But Kory," he stammered, "if you're with Ian, who is with Justin?"

"I am!" Scrubby announced, emerging from the thick bushes. "Scrubby's my name."

"You don't look like Kory," Hector said.

"That's because he's a *tiger*," Kory snarled. "Look closely! See? Tigers have *stripes*." Kory made lines in the air with one paw. "Leopards have *spots!*" He dotted the air with his paw.

One by one, the monkeys seemed to grasp the concept that Kory, Scrubby, Ian, and Justin were four separate creatures. They made a monkey chain and lowered Justin to the ground next to Scrubby and then began jumping up and down, hooting and howling and shaking branches. Leaves floated down around the boys and cats.

As their newfound discovery seeped into their brains, the monkeys began to calm down. However, the branches continued to shake. Ian looked down and saw the leaves on the ground trembling up and down. Justin and Scrubby and Ian and Kory felt the ground rumble beneath their feet.

"Over here!" Kory growled, grabbing Ian and ducking behind the trunk of the tree the monkeys were in.

"What is it?" Scrubby asked.

"No time to explain!" Kory yelled. "Get Justin and get over here *now!*"

Scrubby snatched Justin by his shirttail and leaped behind the tree. He and Justin peered around one side of the tree while Kory and Ian peered around the other side of the tree. The monkeys were actually quiet as they looked at the ground and then at each other.

Binky and his buddies crashed out of the bushes and onto the path. They trundled down the path a few yards past the tree. Suddenly, Binky stopped and sniffed the air. He looked around and sniffed again. He snorted and bellowed, shaking his horns. His eyes narrowed as he searched for the source of the scent he detected.

"I smell a human and a leopard!" he grumbled to his buddies, but loud enough for Ian and Kory to hear. The other water buffaloes sniffed the air, too, nodding their heads in agreement with Binky. Binky took another huge sniff then bellowed, "I smell another human and some other cat, too! *More* humans in *my* jungle? I'll not stand for it! *Do you hear me, humans?*" Binky snorted again, and then stomped down the path. The other water buffaloes followed him, snorting menacingly.

Justin's eyes were as big as saucers. He looked at Scrubby. The tiger looked at Justin and swallowed a big gulp.

Kory let out a big sigh of relief. "Whew, that was a close one," he said. He stepped out from behind the tree.

"W-w-who were they?" Justin asked. He and Scrubby stayed behind the tree.

"Just the local bullies," Ian said. "Binky the water buffalo and his buddies. They're out having a great time terrorizing the jungle."

"Binky doesn't sound like a very tough name," Justin said. "I guess if my name was Binky, I'd be mad, too!" Scrubby snickered and Justin began to laugh. So did Kory and Ian. The monkeys, who had been unusually quiet, began laughing too, even though they didn't know what was so funny.

Kory had planned on taking Justin and Scrubby to the pool and buffalo berry bushes. But Binky was going in that direction, so Kory changed his plans. He whispered something to Ian and Ian nodded excitedly. They turned around and began walking. Scrubby and Justin followed as closely as they could.

"Hey!" Mason yelled. "You just came from that direction!" None of the other monkeys seemed to notice that minor detail.

"We've had a change of plans," Kory said. "We're going someplace else." He looked at Ian and muttered, "But I don't recall it being any of their business!"

Mason sprang from the tree onto Kory's back. In a flash, he was standing in front of him. He took Kory's cheeks in his hands and stared into Kory's eyes.

"May we please go with you?" he pleaded. His monkey eyes grew big and sad. Ian suppressed a giggle. Kory looked around and saw Justin and Scrubby looking at him with big puppy-dog eyes. As if on cue, Hector and the other monkeys hopped down in front of Kory and gave him the big, sad-eyed look.

I'm going to regret this, Kory thought. "Okay," he said. "But this place isn't a place to act goofy. You have to be quiet." Mason and the monkeys nodded. Mason pretended to zip his lips. The other monkeys copied him, zipping each other's lips. Hector zipped Mason's lips again.

"Wait," Mason said, holding up a hand. "Hector, you just unzipped my lips!" He zipped his lips again and looked at Kory. "Mer, mafs medder!"

Kory stared at Mason and sighed deeply. Ian and Justin giggled. This was going to be entertaining, no matter where they were going.

"Let's go before I change my mind," Kory said. He and Ian started walking down the path, followed by Justin and Scrubby. The monkeys took turns hopping back and forth over Scrubby. Scrubby and Justin laughed until their sides began to hurt.

They didn't realize how far they had walked until Kory turned around and said, "We're here! Justin, you and Scrubby come here, but be really quiet." Justin and Scrubby nodded as they walked up to Kory. Kory and Ian softly pushed away branches from a bush and let Justin and Scrubby peer in. Immediately their eyes grew wide in wonder and amazement. Kory smiled at Ian.

"Welcome to the special place," Ian whispered. Justin and Scrubby didn't seem to hear Ian. Mason and his troop took it as an invitation for them, too. Five monkey heads popped up quietly around Justin and Scrubby, and ten monkey eyes grew wide as they took in the sight. Five monkey mouths opened in amazement, but with repeated threatening stares from Kory, they kept quiet.

"Can we go in?" Justin whispered softly to Kory.

"Yes, but slowly and quietly" Kory whispered back. He shot the monkeys a serious look, and they nodded, zipping their lips again in slow motion.

Ian looked at Kory and they smiled. "Go on," Ian whispered to Justin. Justin and Scrubby stole quietly into the meadow. The monkeys held open the branches as Kory and Ian entered, and then crept in behind them. They were careful not to let the branches pop back quickly like a slamming door.

"Okay," Ian whispered, "just start walking slowly. Justin and Scrubby did, walking toward the meadow that looked like a mosaic rainbow with the thousands of butterflies flitting around in it. As the group moved forward, butterflies were stirred up like dust. A big, orange butterfly landed on Scrubby's nose. As he looked at it, his eyes crossed and Justin began to laugh. Instead of flying away, butterflies began landing on Justin. Their legs tickled and this made him laugh more. More butterflies landed on him. In fact, the more he laughed, the more he became covered in butterflies.

Justin's laughter caught on. Ian began to laugh, and soon he was covered head to toe in butterflies. Soon everyone was laughing and butterflies came from everywhere and landed on boys, monkeys, and big cats. They all looked like butterfly topiaries.

Scrubby began to run through the meadow, watching the butterflies explode away from him and then band together and follow him. Ian and Justin took off too, running as fast as they could through the field of butterflies. Butterflies followed them like streams of ribbons. Kory bounded past them and caught up with Scrubby. The two cats leaped in the air with the butterflies rising and falling with their jumps.

Justin looked ahead and saw the crystal blue lake. "Scrubby," he whispered, "there's a lake!" Justin pointed to the lake and a huge grin spread across the tiger's face.

"Let's go!" Scrubby exclaimed. His loud voice sent butterflies streaming into the air, but they quickly landed on the tiger again.

"I've got an idea," Kory said. "Let's race to the lake! Hop on, Ian!" He stopped quickly, and Ian carefully shooed butterflies away from Kory's back and then hopped on quickly before they could land on Kory's back again.

"You're on!" Justin said. He waved away the butterflies and clambered onto Scrubby's back. Scrubby walked over and stood next to Kory.

"I'll start the race," Mason announced. He walked over to the cats and stood in front of them, with Kory on his left and Scrubby on his right. "On your mark ..." he started. Both cats twitched with excitement. "Get set ..." Mason continued. Ian crouched low over Kory's shoulders and dug his heels into Kory's ribs. "*Gold* is my favorite color!"

Kory and Scrubby leaped away in a false start. They stopped as quickly as they had started. Justin bounced up onto Scrubby's head. Mason and the other four monkeys rolled on the ground in laughter.

"That really faked 'em out!" Hector giggled. The monkeys slapped their legs and gave each other high fives. Justin began to giggle as he watched them. Butterflies impatiently flitted around in circles, waiting for the race.

Kory and Scrubby walked back to the starting line. Scrubby was smiling, and in spite of himself, Kory was too. Did he really think Mason would be serious about anything?

"Okay, okay, I'll be serious this time," Mason said. "On your mark ..." Mason started and then began to giggle. "Get set ..." he said as he giggled more. "*Goats* have creepy eyes!" Kory and Scrubby just looked at him. They had both expected this, so neither one flinched when Mason tried to trick them the second time. It didn't matter to the monkeys. Mason and the other monkeys exploded with laughter, slapped each other on the back, and gave more high fives. Kory focused his eyes on the lake. Nothing was between him and the lake except a sea of butterflies and flowers.

Ian remembered the goat at the pumpkin patch. He laughed and said, "Mason's right about goats. I don't mind if you and Scrubby eat goats!"

Mason stood up and pretended to wipe the smile from his face. He looked at Kory and Ian, and then Scrubby and Justin. He giggled once, took a deep breath, and then screeched "*Go!*"

Both cats took off, running as fast as they could. They were running so fast that the butterflies couldn't keep up with them. As they bounded through the meadow, butterflies flitted up and out of the way, regrouping into a colorful cloud that followed behind the cats and boys.

The cats were neck and neck. Ian and Justin felt like they were riding the wind, even though they were clinging to the cats. Justin was sitting up on Scrubby, feeling the wind on his face, grinning from ear to ear, and watching the lake get closer and closer. Ian crouched low over Kory's shoulders and felt the leopard inch ahead of the tiger. He could hear the monkeys whooping behind them. The lake was only about twenty feet away. Ian slunk down a little lower and, in a flash, heard Kory's front paws splash the water. Scrubby's landed a split second later, but Ian and Kory had won the race!

"We win!" Ian exclaimed to Justin and Scrubby. He turned to look at them, but they weren't there. Scrubby had kept on running and jumped into the lake. He was now swimming in the lake with Justin on his back, spitting water out of his mouth like a fountain. They clearly weren't concerned about who had won the race.

Ian climbed off Kory's back and stuck his feet in the cool water. Hundreds of tiny, silvery fish immediately swam up to see if his toes were anything they could eat. They tickled his toes, and their tiny mouths touched his feet. Ian giggled and sat down in the water. More fish swam up and soon they were swimming over his legs. Ian looked like a merman, half human and half fish. He stretched out into the water and floated on his back. Soon he was covered in tiny fish.

Kory sat down on the beach and licked his wet paws. He didn't want to get wetter. He watched Scrubby dive down with Justin and then pop up like a whale breaching out of the ocean. He watched Ian floating peacefully, occasionally wiggling his fingers or toes. The tiny fish would dart away then dart back.

Mason, Hector, and the other monkeys arrived. They had no desire to swim, so they began scouring the beach for things to eat or play with. Hector found two, small, round stones and put them over his eyes. All of the monkeys laughed at this, and then they began tumbling around, pulling tails, and hooting.

The butterflies had banded together and looked like a huge cloud. They hovered behind Kory, waiting for everyone to come back to the meadow. A large, purple butterfly landed on the top of Kory's head and stuck out his proboscis to see if Kory had any nectar on him.

All of a sudden, the water around Scrubby and Justin began bubbling. Justin yelled out in fear as something big and gray began to surface next to him.

"Go Scrubby!" Justin screamed. Scrubby swam back to the shore with Justin clinging tightly to him. "Get out of the lake, Ian!" Justin yelled. "Something's out there!" Scrubby whisked past Ian and Kory and headed for the bushes. The monkeys saw the commotion and followed the tiger.

Ian sat up quickly, and the fish darted away. They didn't come back, and Ian knew why as he looked up. Binky and his water buffalo buddies emerged from the lake, snorting and spewing water.

The butterflies turned in unison and headed for the meadow. They flitted and spun in a circle, looking like a beautiful rainbow whirlwind.

Ian hopped onto Kory's back, and Kory raced off. If this were a race, then Scrubby would certainly win this one. He and Justin were almost to the trees. Kory gained on them quickly. They all burst through the bushes and ran down the trail. The monkeys were close behind, swinging from tree to tree.

"Stay out of my jungle!" Binky bellowed from a distance.

Kory stopped running and turned to look behind him. "Wait!" Kory yelled to Scrubby. Scrubby stopped quickly, nearly unseating Justin. He paced back to Kory and stopped. The monkeys were above them in the trees, hooting excitedly.

"Whew!" Ian sighed. "That was a close one! I didn't expect Binky to be in that lake, even though he is a water buffalo!"

"Scrubby, why didn't you attack Binky?" Justin asked. "You're a tiger! He's like a, a cow!"

"But there's four of them and only one of me!" Scrubby answered. "And I didn't want you to get hurt!"

"Scrubby's right," Kory said. "No one needs to be a hero. There's not much that is more dangerous than an angry water buffalo!"

Justin decided to change the subject. Everyone seemed to have calmed down. "Let's find a snack!" he said.

"How about some buffalo berries?" Ian asked. "They're really good, and hopefully we won't run into Binky anymore!"

Mason shrieked excitedly when he heard Ian say buffalo berries. He and the rest of his troop took off for the pool, shrieking with excitement.

"This way," Kory said. Scrubby followed him. Justin looked behind them occasionally to make sure they weren't being followed by Binky. They weren't.

Ian's stomach began to growl about the time they reached the pool and buffalo berry bushes. He hopped off Kory and ran to pick some berries. Justin saw them too. He slid off Scrubby and ran over to try a berry.

Ian saw a plump, purple berry. He plucked it off the bush and handed it to Justin. Justin looked at it and then popped it into his mouth. He chomped down on the berry and smiled as cool, syrupy juice squirted out. This was the sweetest berry he had ever tasted.

"It's delicious!" he said. He began picking berries and eating them.

Mason and the other monkeys had already stripped one bush of its berries. They were busy at another one. Their faces were a brilliant purple. Justin laughed at them.

"Look at your face," Ian giggled. Justin walked over to the pool and looked at his reflection. He had a nice purple smile and pretty purple teeth. Suddenly his reflection rippled and a tiger's face appeared.

"Hello Justin!" Scrubby said. "Care for a dip in the pool?"

"Don't mind if I do!" Justin said. He jumped in and saw several fish swim away. "Come on in, Ian!" Justin said.

"Okay," Ian answered. He popped one more berry into his mouth and then clambered up the rocks to the ledge where Kory was laying. "Cannonball!" he yelled. He jumped off the ledge and tucked into a ball, splashing into the water.

"Great idea!" Justin said. He climbed up the rocks, but an orange blur streaked past him and catapulted off the ledge ahead of him. Scrubby liked the idea of jumping off the ledge as much as the boys did. Kory watched them with a contented smile on his face. He laid his head on his paws and closed his eyes.

The boys and the tiger jumped and swam until they could barely move. *It is time for more buffalo berries,* Ian thought. He walked slowly over to the bush and sat down beneath it, reaching up only to grab berries.

Justin thought he might eat a few more berries too. He sat down next to Ian and resumed his snacking. Scrubby shook himself off and then sat down next to Kory to lick his paws while Kory dozed. The monkeys were full of berries and napped in a tree next to the buffalo berry bushes. For once, they were quiet. The pool settled back down, and the fish swam to the surface.

Ian and Justin ate and smacked and crunched berries. "These are sure good, Ian!" Justin said. "Thanks for bringing me to the jungle with you and showing me all of the things I saw today. Except for Binky, of course."

"You're welcome," Ian said. "It's more fun with you and Scrubby!"

Justin spied an especially large buffalo berry. It was so purple it was almost black. It was bigger than a quarter. *I bet it's really sweet,* he thought. He reached up and grabbed it. He pulled, but it didn't come off the branch. He pulled harder but the berry wouldn't budge.

"Let me help you," Ian said. The boys stood up. Justin grabbed the berry and began to pull as hard as he could. Ian pulled the branch away so Justin could get his other hand on the berry.

The berry snorted and a face with beady eyes appeared. It wasn't a berry! Justin was pulling on Binky's nose! Binky snorted again and blew Justin's hands off his nose. Justin froze in fear, too scared to scream. Ian froze in fear too, still holding the branch away from Binky's face.

Binky seemed to not notice Ian. He snorted again, and his snort got the attention of Scrubby and Kory.

"*Hey!*" Scrubby said, leaping across the pool to the ground. "*Leave my Justin alone!*"

Kory saw Binky step through the bush toward Justin. Binky shook his horns menacingly at Justin. "One boy in my jungle is bad enough," Binky said coldly. "But I definitely won't stand

for *two* boys in my jungle!" He pawed the ground ready to charge.

Kory leaped down and crept up behind Ian. "Let go of the branch," he whispered. He nudged Ian with his paw.

Ian became aware of what was happening. Justin was in trouble! Suddenly all of his fear vanished.

"Oh, Binky," Ian said calmly.

Binky turned his head to look at Ian. "You're next," he said. "Get ready."

At this distraction, Scrubby grabbed Justin by the shirttail and jerked him away from the water buffalo. Binky turned and saw that Scrubby had Justin. He looked back at Ian and narrowed his eyes. "I don't care who I start with," he said.

Ian let go of the branch, and it snapped back, like a spring, right into Binky's face. *Whap!*

"Ow!" Binky wailed.

Ian grabbed the branch again and let it hit Binky in the face a second time.

Smack!

"My eyes!" the water buffalo moaned. "I think I'm blind!" He rubbed his face on his front legs. When he lifted his head, Ian released the branch a third time.

Whack!

The branch stung as it hit Binky's face. The remaining berries burst on his face, making large purple splotches to go with the red welts from the branch.

"Stop it!" Binky said. He began to cry. "That really hurts! Why are you being so mean to me?" He cried harder. His buddies burst through the bushes and saw their fearless leader bawling like a calf. They began to laugh at him. The commotion woke up the monkeys. When they saw a bruised and berry-stained water buffalo bully crying, they began to laugh too.

"You're the one who is being mean!" Ian said. "Ever since I came to this jungle, you've bullied me around and spoiled my fun. But I will not allow you to pick on my little brother! No more, Binky! You're a bad water buffalo and no one likes you!"

Binky sobbed harder. One of the other water buffaloes turned and kicked dust onto Binky. He certainly didn't want to get whacked with a buffalo berry bush branch by a young boy. He turned and trotted off into the jungle, followed by the other two water buffaloes. Clearly, Binky was no longer their leader.

Binky bawled and bawled. "I'm sorry!" he said. He looked at Ian and his bottom lip quivered.

"Okay," Ian said. "Just remember no one likes a bully. If you're so tough, why don't you pick on someone your own size?"

"That's not fun!" Binky bawled. "And you are right. No one likes me! And now the other water buffaloes don't even like me!" He sat down and cried even harder. The monkeys hopped down from the tree and gathered around Binky.

Ian reached out and patted Binky on the shoulder. "You don't have to be mean," he said. "Everyone will like you if you're nice to them."

"They will?" Binky asked. His eyes stung from the branch whacking them and from his salty tears.

"Sure they will," Kory said. "We'll all like you if you're nice to us and don't try to charge us anymore!"

"You will?" Binky said sheepishly. "You'll be my friends?"

"Sure!" Scrubby said. "Everyone needs friends!" He rubbed up against Binky and nuzzled him. Kory got on the other side and nuzzled him too. Ian and Justin climbed on his back and gave him a big hug.

"See," Justin said. "We're friends now!"

"Thanks, guys!" Binky said, smiling. He had stopped crying. "My dad was the leader of a herd of water buffalo. I guess I thought you had to be mean to get others to do what you wanted."

"Was he mean?" Justin asked.

"Oh no, he was very kind to me," Binky said. "I saw him get stern with a young bull once, and I guess I thought that's how you got others to listen to you. I'm really sorry. I want to be nice!"

"Then let's start fresh now!" Kory said. "You can let the boys ride you back to my tree. It's time for them to go home."

"So soon?" Binky asked.

"They'll be back," Kory said. "I promise." The monkeys made a monkey chain again and lifted the boys onto Binky's back.

"Okay," Binky said. "Let's go." He lumbered off down the path toward Kory's tree. The monkeys hopped lightly onto his back and hitched a ride too. There was plenty of room for them on Binky's broad back.

When they got to Kory's tree, the monkeys sprang up into it. "Bye, boys!" they hooted. "Thanks for letting us hang out with you!" They waved and scampered off in search of bananas.

"Good-bye!" Ian and Justin yelled in unison. They waved to the monkeys, but the monkeys were already gone.

Ian and Justin slid off Binky's back. Ian climbed onto Kory. Justin pulled a buffalo berry out of his pocket and gave it to Binky. He smiled at the huge water buffalo and then climbed onto Scrubby's back.

"Will you let me know when you come back to the jungle?" Binky asked.

"Sure," Ian said. "I promise!" Kory began making his way to the top of the tree. "Bye, Binky!" Ian called out.

"I promise too!" Justin said. He waved to Binky as Scrubby disappeared through the bushes.

Neither boy saw a single tear slide down the now-happy water buffalo face.

Kory and Scrubby came through the wall at the same time. Justin slid off Scrubby and gave the big tiger a big hug.

"I love you, Scrubby," Justin whispered.

"Me too," Scrubby answered. "See you later."

Justin yawned and headed for his bed. He stopped at Ian's door and turned around. All he saw was a painted tiger on Ian's wall. He went to his room, climbed into bed, and promptly fell asleep.

Ian plopped into his bed. "Whew, that was some trip!" he said.

"Yes, it was," Kory said. "You were very brave, Ian. I'm proud of you!" He nuzzled Ian. "See you next time!"

Ian closed his eyes for a moment. When he opened them, he saw a painted leopard watching over him. *If I can stand up to an angry water buffalo, maybe I can stand up to Doug,* he thought. He closed his eyes and drifted off to sleep.

Ian Confronts Doug

It was Monday and the last week of school before Christmas break. Ian's class was having a Christmas party on Friday. "Okay, everyone," Mrs. Land said. "I want each one of you to come up to my desk and draw a name out of the basket. You will buy a gift for that person. Remember, there is a five-dollar limit on the gifts!"

I hope I don't get Doug's name, Ian thought. He could tell by the faces of the kids drawing names that they didn't get Doug's name. There were only five kids left, but at least it was Ian's turn. He walked up to Mrs. Land's desk and stuck his hand into the basket. He wrapped his fingers around a piece of paper and pulled it out. Slowly, he opened it and looked at the name. *Mollie!* Trying to maintain a straight face, he suppressed a smile and put the paper in his pocket.

Doug was next. He stomped up to Mrs. Land's desk and shoved his hand into the basket. He pulled out all of the names and opened them up. His name was still in there, so were Ian's, Ginger's and Tristan's.

"Only get one name, please, Doug," Mrs. Land reminded him. She sighed a heavy sigh. She couldn't wait for Christmas break.

Doug kept Ian's name and crumpled the paper into his hand. He stuffed the piece of paper into his mouth and looked at Ian.

"Get that paper out of your mouth, Doug!" Mrs. Land scolded him. "You're not a goat!" Everyone giggled at that thought.

Doug walked over to the trashcan and spit the paper into the can. It missed and landed on the floor. Doug didn't bother to pick it up. He didn't know Mrs. Land was watching him.

"Please pick up that piece of paper, Doug," Mrs. Land said. "No one needs to pick up something that has been in your mouth." Mrs. Land sighed. "Only five more days," she whispered quietly.

Doug bent down and picked up the wet paper. He flung it into the trashcan and it stuck to the side.

When everyone had finished drawing names, Mrs. Land began passing out two sheets of green construction paper and one sheet of red construction paper to everyone. "Today we are going to make Christmas wreaths!" Mrs. Land said. "I want you to trace your hands on the green paper. Try to trace your hands on the paper as many times as you can. Then we will cut out the hands and make the wreath! The red paper is for a bow and holly berries."

What a great idea, Ian thought. He began tracing his hands. "My mom will hang this on the front door or use it for a centerpiece," he told Tristan. "This is going to be fun! I can't wait to show my mom this wreath!"

Everyone, including Doug, got busy making their wreaths. Mrs. Land walked around and helped them trace their hands that they didn't write with so their wreaths would be made of their left hands and right hands.

When everyone was finished cutting out their handprints, Mrs. Land gave each child a circle cut out of a thick paper plate.

"Glue your handprints on the circle," she said. "When you are finished with that, I'll help you cut out bows and berries." She held up a hole punch. "We'll use this to make the berries," she said.

By the time everyone finished their wreaths, it was time for lunch. "Write your name on the back of your wreath, and then we'll wash our hands before lunch. The weather is nice enough to go outside today for recess. But take your coats!" Everyone lined up and walked to the bathroom to wash their hands. As they got back in line to go to the cafeteria, Doug raised his hand.

"Yes, Doug," Mrs. Land said.

"I forgot my lunch," Doug said. "It's in the room."

"Go get it and meet us in the cafeteria," Mrs. Land said.

Doug turned around and walked to the room. When he got in the room, he grabbed his lunch, and then spied the scissors in his desk. He picked up the scissors and walked over to Ian's wreath. He picked up the wreath and began cutting fingers off. Little, green fingers floated onto Ian's desk and the floor. He was so busy cutting the fingers off Ian's wreath that he didn't notice Ian walking into the room. He had forgotten his milk money in his backpack.

"What are you doing to my wreath?" Ian exclaimed when he saw Doug cutting off the fingers.

Doug jumped at the sound of Ian's voice and stared at him, wild-eyed. He had been caught! Quickly he put the scissors in his right pocket and glared at Ian.

"You better not tell Mrs. Land!" he said, "Or else!"

"Or else what?" Ian said. "You'll hit me or think of some other way to terrorize me or the other kids?" Ian turned around and raced down the hall, forgetting all about his milk money.

When he got to the cafeteria, he found Mrs. Land and told her what had happened. "Follow me," she told Ian.

They turned around to go to the classroom just as Doug walked into the cafeteria, swinging his lunchbox like nothing had happened. He stopped when he saw Ian and Mrs. Land walking toward him. Everyone in the cafeteria stopped eating and talking.

"Did you cut the fingers off Ian's wreath?" Mrs. Land said, putting her hands on her hips. "Ian said he caught you."

"He's lying!" Doug said. "He just wants me to get into trouble!"

Ian tapped Mrs. Land on her arm. "He's got the scissors in his pocket," he said.

"Is that true, Doug?" Mrs. Land asked.

"No!" Doug lied.

"Let me see, then," Mrs. Land demanded.

Doug shoved his hand into his left pocket and swirled his hand around in it. When he pulled his hand out, it was empty. "See!" he said, sneering at Ian.

"What about the other pocket?" Mrs. Land said calmly.

The sneer melted from Doug's face. Slowly he put his hand into his other pocket. Mrs. Land could see the scissors poking into Doug's jeans. He pulled out his hand and had the scissors in them.

"Come with me," Mrs. Land told Doug. "You get to explain everything to Mrs. Carter."

Ian turned and walked over to the table. He sat down to eat, although he wasn't very hungry. His wreath was ruined, and

Doug was probably going to beat him up! He didn't have time to dwell on that thought, though. All of his friends demanded to know what happened, so Ian told them the story.

"You actually caught Doug?" Alan said in disbelief.

"And you stood up to him, *and then told on him?*" Mollie asked. "How brave," she whispered quietly and then smiled at Ian.

"Yes, but now he's going to beat me up!" Ian said.

"Well, he won't right now," Reed said laughing a little. "He's busy explaining everything to Mrs. Carter, including why he lied to Mrs. Land! I'd love to be a little mouse in that office!"

Ian laughed. Reed was always good for making everyone laugh, no matter what the situation might be.

"Well, I say we take advantage of the playground without Doug," Ginger said. "Eat up everyone, so we can go outside and play in peace!"

Ian ate his lunch. He felt better with his friends supporting him. And outside, it was wonderful without Doug lurking around.

"Too bad it can't be like this all of the time," Ian said to Tristan. Tristan nodded in agreement.

After a while, Mrs. Land came outside and blew her whistle for her class to line up. Doug was not with her. On the way into the school, Mrs. Land told Ian that he could make another wreath that afternoon. Ian smiled at her and told her thanks.

When they got back into the classroom, Mrs. Land told them to take out their reading books. As the children got out their books, they managed to look over at Ian's desk to see just how bad his wreath was. It was indeed pitiful. Little green fingers were strewn all over the floor.

As the class did their reading assignment, Mrs. Land

brought over more construction paper for Ian. "We'll have some free time later, and you can work on your wreath," she told Ian.

After they finished their story and questions, Mrs. Land told the class they would have thirty minutes of free time. "You need to read a library book or draw," she said. "And you need to stay quiet."

Ian traced his hands quickly, but not too quickly. He didn't want to make his hands look stubby and fat. Tristan and Mollie helped him cut out the handprints. Mollie smiled at Ian. "I'll help you cut out berries too," she said.

"Thanks," Ian said, smiling at her.

By the time free time was over, Ian had made another wreath, and he thought it looked better than the first one. "May I keep my wreath on your desk until it's time to go home, Mrs. Land?" Ian asked.

"Certainly," Mrs. Land answered. "Lay it right here on my grade book."

Ian walked up to Mrs. Land's desk and put his wreath on top of her grade book. He turned around and walked back to his desk. Doug walked in the door and looked at Ian.

He looks like he's been crying, Ian thought. *Good.*

When Doug sat down, Mrs. Land told him what story to read. "You may need to take the questions home and answer them if you don't get finished," she said. Doug took out his book and opened to the story. He stared at the pages, as if he was expecting the characters to spring from the book and tell him the story.

"Okay, class," Mrs. Land said. "While Doug reads his story, you may continue to read or draw. When Doug finishes his story, we'll take another short recess outside. It's too nice of a day for December to not enjoy the outdoors. Then we'll come in and do a little bit of math and then get ready to go home."

Everyone looked at Doug. He was actually reading the story and answering a few questions as he went. He finished the story and questions ten minutes later and closed his book.

"Okay," Mrs. Land announced, "let's go outside. Be sure and take your coats."

Everyone grabbed their coats and lined up. Reed was the line leader, so he led everyone out to the playground. Kids scattered like leaves in the wind.

Ian, Alan, Tristan, and Reed headed for the slide. Ian climbed to the top of the slide and looked around for Mollie. She and Ginger were going to the swings. He slid down and ran around to get in line. Tristan was ahead of him. Reed and Alan were sliding down together, taking their time.

"Hurry up!" Tristan said. Reed and Alan laughed. They slid down even more slowly.

By the time Reed and Alan reached the ground and Tristan was starting to slide down the slide, Ian was at the top of the slide. He looked toward the swings and saw Mollie. She was swinging up high. Then Ian saw Doug walking up behind her. *I hope she bumps into him and knocks him down,* Ian thought.

Mollie didn't even notice that Doug was behind her. As she swung back, he grabbed the swing. Mollie lurched forward. She fell out of the swing, but managed to hang onto the chain so she didn't hit the ground. She froze when she saw Doug staring coldly at her.

"*Hey!*" Ian shouted from the top of the slide. "*Leave Mollie alone!*" He slid down the slide and hit the ground running. He raced over to the swing and stood between Mollie and Doug. "Why don't you leave *everyone* alone?" Ian yelled at Doug.

"What if I don't want to?" Doug yelled back. "What are you gonna do about it? Tell on me?" Doug took a step toward Ian and pushed him. It was a hard push, and Ian fell backward onto the ground.

Mrs. Land had seen Ian race across the playground toward the swings. When she saw Doug at the swings, she knew something was going to happen. And she was right. She saw Doug push Ian down. What she wasn't ready for was Ian to get up quickly and push Doug back. Doug wasn't ready for it, either. His knees buckled under him.

"Oommppff," he groaned as his bottom hit the ground. Dead grass and dust puffed into the air around him.

Mrs. Land blew her whistle as loudly as she could. She hurried over to the swings. Everyone stopped to see where she was going. When she got to the swings, Ian was standing over Doug. Doug looked scared. A big tear slid down his cheek. He wiped it off quickly, hoping no one saw it. Mollie was standing behind Ian. Soon all of the kids had raced over to the swings and made a circle around Ian and Doug.

"Get up, Doug!" Mrs. Land said. "We're going inside. And, Doug, you and Ian are going to Mrs. Carter's office. You can stay in there until school is out, and then you and your parents can talk to Mrs. Carter and me." She marched the kids into the classroom, and then watched as Ian and Doug walked down the hall to Mrs. Carter's office.

While Ian and Doug waited for Mrs. Carter to talk to them, Ian kept thinking about how much trouble he was going to be in at home. But then he thought about Mollie and what if she had been seriously hurt. Angry tears filled his eyes. He closed his eyes tightly until he felt the tears disappear. What were Mom and Dad going to say—or do—to him? Ian said a silent prayer that his parents wouldn't kill him.

Ian opened his eyes and looked over at Doug. Doug had lots of big tears running down his face, but he didn't seem to care. *Two trips to the office in one day,* Ian thought. *Doug must have just set a record.* He glared at Doug. He had so many reasons to be mad at him. Doug had done so many things to him and the other kids. *Maybe Doug will finally be expelled,* Ian thought.

Doug looked at Ian, and his eyes grew wide. Fresh tears welled up in his eyes and spilled out. His bottom lip quivered. He wiped his nose on his sleeve, and then buried his head in his hands.

After what seemed like an eternity, the bell rang. The hallway was filled with the sounds of happy children leaving for the day. In a few minutes, Mom and Justin walked into the office.

"You got sent to the principal's office?" Justin exclaimed.

"Be quiet, Justin!" Ian snapped. "I had a good reason!"

Mom told Justin to sit in the hallway and watch the goldfish in the tank. Justin was happy to do that. "Don't tap on the glass, though," she said.

"I won't," Justin said. As he walked out, Doug's mother came in the office. She was carrying Doug's baby sister. The baby saw Doug and smiled a big smile. Doug looked at his mother and started crying out loud.

A few minutes later, Mrs. Land came in and knocked on Mrs. Carter's door. "We're here," she said.

Mrs. Carter opened her office door and told everyone to come in. When everyone was in, she closed the door. "Who would like to tell me what happened?" she said.

"I will," Mrs. Land said. She told Mrs. Carter what she had seen. Doug's mother began to cry softly. Doug reached over and patted her hand. He was still crying.

"You boys know that fighting is not allowed at school," Mrs. Carter said.

Great, Ian thought. *I'm going to get expelled too. What if I'm not accepted to any other school? I'll be a third grade dropout! I can't go to college! I can't support a family!* His mind raced with wild thoughts. Suddenly Ian jumped up and looked at Mrs. Carter.

"Please don't expel me, Mrs. Carter!" Ian pleaded. "Doug has done so many things to me, like breaking my crayons, smashing my cookies, putting a thumbtack in my chair, and cutting the fingers off of my wreath! He picks on the other kids too, and today at the swings, Mollie could have been hurt really badly when he jerked her out of the swing! He's so mean!" *Whew!* He hadn't planned on saying all of that, but was glad he did. He sat down, and Mom put her arm around him. Ian looked at Doug. He wasn't afraid of him anymore. He knew standing up for Mollie was the right thing to do.

Doug cried harder. "I'm supposed to be tough!" he wailed. "That's what my dad told me to do. He said I need to be in charge and be the man of the house while he's …" Doug's voice trailed off. He closed his mouth and softly sobbed. Ian wasn't expecting that reaction.

Doug's mother wiped her eyes. She looked at Ian and Mom.

"I'm sorry for the way Doug has acted," she said. "His father has a serious illness. He hasn't been able to work, and things have been really tough on us. I think they've been the toughest on Doug. His father isn't able to do things with Doug like he used to." She paused to wipe her nose. "He told Doug that he would have to be the man of the house for a while. He said men had to be tough as nails. I think Doug was confused. Even though his father is a good man and not mean at all, I think Doug misunderstood." She began to cry.

Mom handed her a tissue and patted her on the knee. "Doug is not a mean boy," she continued. "I think he has some anger built up inside him. He has to help me out with the chores and taking care of the baby. He doesn't have much time for fun. I think he's resentful of the other kids and took his anger out on them. I'm really sorry about all of the things he's done. I haven't even told his father about the incidents at school, because I didn't want him to feel worse or worry."

"I wish you would have told us," Mrs. Land said. "Perhaps we could have helped Doug if we had known about your circumstances." She looked at Doug and her face softened.

"I'll try to find another school for Doug during the Christmas break," Doug's mother said. "Maybe things will be better if he changes schools. Now that I know why he's behaving this way, maybe I can help him."

Suddenly Ian stood up. "Doug doesn't have to change schools!" he said. He couldn't believe that he had actually said that. *Must be a fever,* he thought. "Doug," Ian said, looking Doug squarely in the eyes, "do you promise to be nice? I know that if you're nice to everyone, they'll be nice to you, even if things aren't going very well. That's what friends do!"

Mom reached out and grabbed Ian's hand. Her eyes filled with tears. She was so proud of Ian for trying to help Doug.

"Thank you, Ian," Mrs. Carter said. Her eyes had tears in them, too. "I think Doug can stay at this school. Changing schools may not be a good idea right now. I bet he makes some new friends quickly!" She winked at Ian and then Doug.

Doug smiled at Mrs. Carter. He looked at Ian and then stood up. He reached out his right hand and grabbed Ian's right hand.

"Thanks, Ian," he said. "I promise I'll be nice. I'm sorry I was so mean to you and the other kids. I wish there was a way I could make it up to you."

Ian looked at Doug. Doug was being sincere. Ian swallowed a big lump in his throat. "Just be a good friend," Ian said. "That will help your mom and dad the most. And," Ian continued, smiling, "don't give any more haircuts to my wreath!"

Doug saw Ian smiling. "It's a deal!" he said.

Mrs. Land gave Doug a big hug. "It will be nice to have the *real* Doug at school tomorrow," she said.

"Thank you so much," Doug's mother said. She looked at Ian and smiled. "Thank you most of all, Ian," she said softly. Doug and his mother and baby sister left Mrs. Carter's office.

"Mrs. Land," Ian said, "I think I have a good idea for the Christmas party. It's a little different then what we had planned." Ian told Mrs. Land, Mrs. Carter, and Mom his idea. They agreed that it was a great idea indeed.

"I'll send a note home with everyone tomorrow," Mrs. Land said. "I'm so proud of you, Ian. You solved this problem as well as Solomon would have. I'll see you tomorrow."

Ian and Mom left Mrs. Carter's office and found Justin staring at the fish. He was bugging out his eyes and had his cheeks sucked in, making a fish face at the fish. They didn't seem to notice or care.

At home, Mom told Dad what had happened. Dad gave Ian a big hug and told him he was a good boy and would be a good man. Ian went to bed feeling good about everything. He actually couldn't wait to get to school tomorrow and see the new and improved Doug. Everyone was going to be in for a surprise!

The next few days passed quickly, and finally it was Friday, the day of the Christmas party. Ian woke up early and got dressed. He couldn't wait until he got to school! They only had to go a half of a day, but that wasn't what was so exciting to Ian. Today would be the best school Christmas party ever! He and Mom had made Christmas cookies last night. Mom grabbed the tray of cookies, and Ian got his Christmas gift for the party.

When they got to school, many of the other kids had gotten there early, too. Everyone was so excited. They couldn't believe how nice Doug actually had been the past three days. He was really fun to be around.

"This is going to be a great party," Alan said. "I wonder where Doug is?"

"Hopefully he'll be here," Ginger said.

"He will," Ian said, secretly hoping he was right.

A few minutes later, Doug walked in carrying his gift for the gift exchange. Everyone smiled at him when he came in the room. He smiled back as he hung up his coat and then sat down at his desk.

"Well, today is a very special day," Mrs. Land said. "It's our Christmas party, as all of you know. I think we need to start it early, like, now!" Everyone cheered and clapped. "So let's play some games, and then we'll open our gifts and then eat!" she said. "After that, it will be time to go home!"

The kids played games, like Pin the Tail on the Reindeer, sang a few Christmas carols, and watched *How the Grinch Stole Christmas*. Soon it was time to open presents.

"Okay, everyone, let's make a big circle with our chairs,"

Mrs. Land said. "That way we can all see each other and see what everyone gets! Tristan, we'll start with you. Then whoever gets your gift will go next."

Tristan stood up and picked up his gift. He walked over to Doug. "I drew your name," he said. He smiled and handed the gift to Doug, then walked back to his chair, and sat down.

Doug unwrapped his gift from Tristan. It was a football. "Thanks, Tristan!" Doug said. "I love to play football!"

"You're welcome, Doug," Tristan said. "Now it's your turn."

Doug picked up his gift and walked over to Ian. "This isn't much," he said. "I hope you like it."

"I will," Ian said. He opened his gift. It was a small, plastic snow globe. Inside was a nativity scene. "Thanks!" Ian exclaimed. "I love snow globes! Did you know I collected them?"

Doug smiled. "No, I didn't know that. I like snow globes too. I liked this one, because Jesus was our gift from God. And you gave me a great gift of friendship, Ian. Thanks!"

Ian didn't know what to say. He smiled at Doug. He thought of the Grinch and how his heart grew so much when he realized what Christmas was really about. "My turn," he said. He picked up his gift sack and walked over to Doug and handed it to him. "Merry Christmas, Doug," he said.

"I already got my gift," Doug said. He looked confused.

"Well, open it anyway," Ian said. "It's for you."

Doug opened the gift sack and pulled out a teddy bear. It was so soft and cuddly. He held it close to him and hugged it.

"Thanks," he said. "I didn't have a teddy bear." Ian gulped at this thought. *Who doesn't have a teddy bear,* he thought.

"Okay, Alan, you're next to Ian," Mrs. Land said. "Why don't you go next?"

Alan nodded. He picked up his gift and walked over to Doug and handed it to him.

"What is this?" Doug said.

"It's for you, Doug," Alan said. "Go ahead and open it!"

Doug opened his gift and found a deck of cards and some puzzle books.

"I thought you and your dad might be able to work some puzzles or play cards," Alan said.

"Yeah, I bet we can do that!" Doug exclaimed.

Ginger was next. She too walked over to Doug and handed him a present. Naturally it was in a pink gift sack with pink tissue paper flowing out of it.

"I hope Doug likes pink!" Reed whispered to Tristan.

Doug pulled out the tissue paper and then reached in and pulled out a pink stuffed pony. He stared at it. "Uh, thanks, Ginger," he said.

"Actually it's for your sister," Ginger said. "Your gift is in there, too."

Doug reached back into the sack and pulled out a sack of marbles. Surprisingly, none of them were pink. "Thanks," he said.

One by one, each child gave Doug a gift. That was Ian's idea. He decided Doug might not have a very good Christmas, since his dad was ill and unable to work for a while. He had asked Mrs. Land if all of the class could get Doug a gift instead of getting one for each other. He had told her that's what Christmas was all about. And everyone had agreed when they got their note from Mrs. Land.

Doug continued opening gifts. He got a soccer ball, board games, movie rental cards, candy, art supplies, and books. Some kids had put small baby toys and clothes for his baby sister in with his gifts. When Doug was finished opening his gifts, Mrs. Land handed him a gift sack. Inside it were gift cards for restaurants, the grocery store, gas station, and an envelope with money in it.

"It's for your parents from the class and their parents," Mrs. Land said smiling. "Merry Christmas, Doug!"

As if on cue, the whole class shouted "*Merry Christmas, Doug!*"

Doug beamed. "Thanks," he said softly. "Thanks for all of the gifts, but mostly, thanks for forgiving me and being my friend!"

"So enough of the gush; let's eat!" Reed said.

Everyone laughed and then lined up to fill their plates with small sandwiches, cookies, fruit, pretzels, and chips. Mrs. Land had made a special Christmas punch. And to Ginger's delight, it was pink!

Doug took his plate over to the window and looked out. He was truly amazed at what had happened today.

Ian saw him and walked over to him. "Did you try one of my Christmas reindeer cookies?" he asked.

"Yes," Doug said. "I found one without broken legs!" He looked at Ian and Ian grinned.

"None of them have broken legs," Ian said. He bit a leg off of his reindeer cookie. "Well, this one does," he said and began to laugh. "Merry Christmas, Doug," Ian said. "I mean it. And I'm praying for your dad."

"Thanks," Doug said. "He's getting better. The doctor said he might be able to go back to work in January."

Ian and Doug looked out the window. Without thinking,

Doug put his arm around Ian and gave him a hug. Then he picked up his reindeer cookie and took a bite. As he did, large snowflakes began to fall.

A Jungle Party

Christmas vacation sped by. Ian had stayed super busy. First, they had Mom's family Christmas at Valerie's house. They spent the night there, and then drove to Rusty's house the next day for Dad's family Christmas. They stayed at Rusty's house for a week. When they got home, Grandy and Pappy wanted the boys to spend a couple of days with them.

Alan had a New Year's party, and Ian went to that, even though the party was over at 10:00, because none of the kids could stay up until midnight. Doug came to the party and was a totally different boy. He smiled, laughed, made jokes, and was pleasant to be around. He told Ian and Alan that his dad was better, and they had been working the puzzle books that Alan gave them for Christmas.

A few days after New Year's Day was Justin's birthday. So naturally, there was a family party that lasted all day, and then Justin had a friend party. He invited three boys over: Trevor, Riley, and Justice. They had planned on eating pizza and cake (and they did) and playing army games. The night before the party, it snowed several inches, so they bundled up and played army games in the snow. They built forts, stockpiled snow-balls, and had a snowball war. Then they built a few snowmen and pelted them with snowballs until nothing was left but a worn out pile of snow. By the time the party was over, there was not a speck of snow in the yard that hadn't been stepped on or turned into a snowball.

And now, it was the last night of Christmas break. Ian was actually excited about starting back to school tomorrow. He couldn't wait to see his friends again. Many of them had been out of town and didn't get to come to Alan's party. Ian was anxious to hear what they got for Christmas. He wondered how many pink things Ginger got. *I bet she had a pink Christmas tree too,* he thought.

"Time for bed," Dad said. They each said a prayer, and then Dad whisked Ian up into his arms and slung him onto his back.

Justin trotted down the hall in front of Dad and then ducked into the laundry room. *"Boo!"* he shouted as Dad and Ian walked by. They had seen him and knew what he was going to do, so they pretended to be scared.

Dad grabbed Justin and scooped him up. He carried him to his bed and softly plopped him down. Mom came in and tucked Justin into bed. She kissed him on the tip of his nose and handed him Scrubby.

Ian was still clinging to Dad's back. It made him think about riding Binky. Dad walked into Ian's room and over to his bed. He turned around and bent down. Ian slid off Dad's back and onto his bed. Mom tucked Ian in and kissed him on his nose too. Dad turned off the lights, and he and Mom left the room.

As they walked down the hall, Ian listened to their footsteps. He turned and looked at the painted Kory on his wall and then stared at the ceiling. Suddenly, he felt something in his bed. It was Justin.

"I'm going to miss you when you go to school tomorrow, Ian," Justin said.

"You have a bunch of new toys to play with," Ian said as he yawned. "That will probably keep you busy."

"I guess so," Justin said as he yawned too. He and Ian both closed their eyes for a minute.

Thump!

Plop!

The boys opened their eyes. Kory and Scrubby were there, smiling down at the boys. "Well, well, look who has decided to come home," Kory said as Ian grabbed him and gave him a big hug.

"Did you forget where you lived?" Scrubby asked Justin. Justin shook his head no and buried it into Scrubby's chest.

"How about taking one more trip?" Kory asked. Ian was already climbing onto Kory's back before Kory could finish his sentence. Justin hopped up and clambered onto Scrubby's back. The big cats leaped into the wall, and when the boys opened their eyes, they were back in the jungle. In an instant, Kory and Ian were on the ground next to Scrubby and Justin.

"Come on," Kory said. "I've got something to show you two!"

"You're going to love it!" Scrubby said.

"Have we been there before?" Ian asked.

"You've been to the place," Kory replied. "But you've never seen it like this."

Ian looked at Justin. Justin shrugged his shoulders.

"Let's go then," he said.

They began walking toward the pool and buffalo berry

bushes. The jungle seemed unusually quiet. Ian didn't notice any birds flying or squawking. *I wonder what's going on,* he thought.

"Here we are," Kory said a few minutes later. As they rounded the curve in the path, the pool came into view.

"*Surprise!*" many thunderous voices yelled at once. Ian and Justin both jumped at the explosion of noise. They saw Binky, his buddies, the monkeys, Exx, Jerry, countless birds, a zebra, a hippo, a rhino, and an ostrich. All of a sudden, from behind the menagerie, hundreds of butterflies glided into the air and spelled *hello*. Even the little silver fish were at the edge of the pool sending their greetings with air bubbles. Now Ian knew why the jungle was so quiet. Everyone was here!

"Are you surprised?" Binky said excitedly as he trotted up to Ian and Justin. "I wanted to do something special for you as a gesture of friendship."

"I sure am," Ian said. "This is quite a party!"

"Thanks!" Binky said. "Come over here with me."

The boys and cats followed Binky to the pool. All around the pool were yummy things to eat. There were wooden bowls stuffed with buffalo berries, bananas, grapes, mangoes, and papayas. One wooden plate was heaped with shredded coconut and another had a variety of nuts piled onto it. Coconut shell cups were filled with various fruit juices. Flowers were strewn everywhere. Butterflies flitted here and there. Colorful parrots perched on trees and flew around.

"I couldn't wait for you to get here," Binky said. "Everyone's been busy gathering food and squishing fruit for the juice. Jerry spent all day cracking nuts. I hope he shares with you!"

Ian looked around and saw Jerry fiercely guarding the plate of nuts. Whenever anyone tried to take a nut off the plate,

Jerry gritted his teeth and growled. He was holding a particularly large Brazil nut in his hands.

"It doesn't look like he's going to share," Justin giggled. "It's a good thing I don't like nuts!"

"No, I haven't seen anyone take a nut," Kory said.

The zebra trotted up to Justin and Ian. "I'm Checkers," he said. "I've heard a lot about you. This is my friend, Sandy," Checkers said. He pointed a hoof to the ostrich, who was walking slowly up behind him. Sandy blinked two huge eyes at the boys, and then hurriedly looked around on the ground, as if she would like to bury her head in the sand.

"It's nice to meet you," Ian and Justin said together.

Ian reached over to grab a banana. The bananas weren't there. He looked over to where the bowl of bananas had been and saw the bowl being lifted up into a tree. Mason, Hector, and the other monkeys had formed a monkey chain to spring down, grab the bananas, and spring back up with their cache. Ian reached for a buffalo berry instead. *I can eat bananas at home,* he thought.

"Before everyone gets too full, let's have a race!" Binky shouted. "Ian, you can ride on me!" He trotted over to Ian and scooped his head under Ian's bottom. He lifted his head and gently flung Ian onto his broad back.

"Okay," Ian said. "I guess I'm riding Binky in the race."

"Now," Binky said, "who will race me?"

"I will," Checkers said, waving his front hooves. "How about it, Justin?"

"Cool," Justin said. "I've never ridden a zebra!"

Checkers walked over to Justin and Justin clambered onto his back. He grabbed Checkers' short mane, ready to race.

"Where are we racing to?" Ian asked Binky.

"How about to my tree and back," Kory said.

"Sounds good," Ian said. "I think the trail is wide enough for all of us, in case it's a neck and neck race."

"But it won't be," Binky whispered. "I'll leave Checkers in the dust!"

"I'll start the race!" Mason shrieked as he bounded out of the tree. He had banana all over his face.

"That's okay," Scrubby said. "I'll do it. It will take too long if you do it!"

Mason shrugged his shoulders, peeled another banana, and popped it into his mouth. He mumbled something, but Scrubby didn't hear it.

One of Binky's buddies drew a line in the sand by the pool. Binky and Checkers walked up to the line. Justin clung to the patch of zebra mane. Ian didn't have anything to hold on to, except big water buffalo shoulders.

"On your mark …" Scrubby began, "Get set—oh, and may the best team win," he added, winking at Justin. "*Go!*"

Binky lumbered off, rumbling down the path. It was barely wide enough for him and the zebra. Checkers dug his hind legs under him and took off like a shot. He zipped past Binky and raced for the tree. Justin was holding on for dear life, almost wishing he was riding a huge, lumbering water buffalo instead of a lightning-fast zebra.

"See ya later!" Checkers called out to Binky as he streaked ahead of Binky in a black and white blur. He sped on until he saw Kory's tree, spun around it in a quick circle, and raced back down the path toward the pool. Binky was trundling along, moving rather quickly for a large beast, but he was really no match for a smaller, quicker zebra.

By the time he circled Kory's tree, Checkers was nearly

back at the pool. Binky kept going. He could hear all of the animals cheering. He was actually having too much fun with his friends to care if he won the race. When Binky and Ian got back to the pool, the animals cheered for them too.

"Congratulations, Checkers," Binky said. "You are *fast!*"

"Thanks," Checkers said. "You're pretty quick for a water buffalo!"

Ian slid off Binky and disappeared into the jungle. He reappeared a few minutes later carrying a vine with pretty purple flowers woven into it. He fastened it around Binky's neck and gave him a big hug!

"You're still a winner!" he said. "The old Binky would have tripped Checkers in order to win the race!"

"The old Binky would have crashed the party!" Binky laughed. "I'm the new and improved Binky!"

Ian laughed. He looked around when he heard splashing. Justin and Scrubby were doing cannonballs into the pool. The monkeys were swinging each other into the pool, and Kory was actually taking a dip. Ian decided to join him. He slipped into the water and swam out to his friend. The hippo had waded into the pool and submerged. Ian noticed that the little silver fish were nowhere to be found. There was also a pretty pink flamingo standing on one leg at the shore of the pool. *I bet his name is Blackie,* Ian thought.

"Quite a party, huh?" Kory said. "Binky has been planning this since you left. He couldn't wait until you came back to the jungle. He insisted I bring you today! And Scrubby was excited when he found out Justin just had a birthday."

"Things are nicer now in the jungle," Ian said. "They are at school too." He told Kory all about Doug. "They remind me of each other," he added. He floated onto his back and spewed

water out of his mouth like a little fountain. Ian noticed an elephant slurping up water through his trunk.

"Excuse me a minute, Kory," he said.

He swam over to the elephant and introduced himself. "Pleased to meet you, Ian," the elephant said. "My name is Tiny." Ian wasn't surprised at his name, but he was surprised when Tiny wrapped his trunk around Ian, lifted him out of the pool and set him on his back. Ian was thrilled. Not only did he get to meet an actual elephant, but he was going to get to ride one as well! He felt like a king as Tiny walked around the party, trumpeting for everyone to notice the boy on his back.

Suddenly the monkeys leaped into a tree. Hector began slapping his hands on a branch. Two other monkeys found hollow reeds and blew into them. Mason had a large, dry gourd he began to shake. The other monkey shook a smaller branch, rustling the leaves.

At the sound of this monkey music, Justin and Scrubby climbed out of the pool and began to dance. Scrubby moved his hips back and forth, and Justin shook and shimmied all over. Soon all of the animals were dancing or clapping along. Jerry even chimed in, but kept a close eye on the plate of nuts. So far, no one had gotten one, and he was going to keep it that way. He couldn't help but swish and twitch his tail to the beat of the music though.

The boys and animals continued to dance, sing, play games, and eat. Eventually, most of the food—except for the nuts— was eaten. Justin yawned, and Kory said it was probably time to go.

"Oh, I hate to leave," Ian said.

"Well, you've got a big day at school tomorrow," Kory added. "You've got a new friend to play with!"

"That's right," Ian said smiling. "I have lots of new friends here and at home!"

"Let's go then," Kory said. "I don't know how we'll top your next trip to the jungle!"

"I always have a good time with you," Ian said, stroking Kory's soft fur. "We don't have to have a party!" He climbed onto Kory's back and Kory started down the trail. Scrubby and Justin followed, although Scrubby was walking very slowly. Justin looked back and noticed all of the animals were following them. What a funny jungle parade!

When they got to the tree, everyone said good-bye to Ian and Justin.

"Thanks for the great party!" Ian called out to them. He slid off Kory's back and walked over to Binky. He wrapped his arms around him and gave him a big hug. "Thanks, Binky!" he said softly.

Binky nuzzled him. "Don't stay away so long," he said.

"I won't," Ian said. He climbed back onto Kory's back, and in one giant leap, Kory was at the top of his tree. Ian turned around and waved to everyone once more. They disappeared as Kory and Ian landed in Ian's bedroom.

Justin and Scrubby burst through the wall humming the monkey music. Justin gave Scrubby a big hug and trotted off to bed. Scrubby peered around Ian's door and watched Justin climb into bed.

Ian gave Kory a huge hug, wrapping his arms tightly around the leopard. He lay back onto his bed. "Thanks for the wonderful party," he whispered.

"You're welcome," Kory said.

Ian closed his eyes and smiled. He opened them quickly, but Kory and Scrubby were gone, back to their painted posts on the wall.

Still smiling, Ian closed his eyes again. He wondered if Doug was as excited about school starting tomorrow as he was. He said a little prayer, thanking God for his friends, and that Doug's dad was better. He drifted off to sleep, anxiously awaiting new adventures at school and in Kory's jungle.